Now is the Hour

Women are meant to be loved,
not to be understood

– Oscar Wilde

Patricia Bragdon

Trenton, Georgia

Print ISBN: 978-1-959621-15-7
Ebook ISBN: 979-8-88531-844-0

Published by BookLocker.com, Inc., Trenton, Georgia.

The characters and events in this book are fictitious. Any similarity to real persons, living or dead, is coincidental and not intended by the author.

BookLocker.com, Inc.
2024

First Edition

Library of Congress Cataloging in Publication Data
Bragdon, Patricia
Now is the Hour by Patricia Bragdon
Library of Congress Control Number: 2024920444

Dedication

For Sufian Zhemukhov and the members of the Writing Workshop, with thanks for the gentle criticism, the encouragement, and the laughter.

Chapter One

Sailing from Sydney, 1965

The great ocean liner *Oriana*, newest of the P&O fleet, trembled a little as the engines throbbed quietly in preparation for the midnight departure from Sydney on her long maiden voyage around the world. Or was it Thalia who was trembling? It was her maiden voyage too. She could feel the movement in her body, in her bones, her hands, the ends of her hair. Was she afraid? She couldn't tell. Did she love this man she was going to marry at the end of this journey? Again, she couldn't tell. She liked him, she knew that much, liked his steadiness and resolve, his curiosity, and his sense of humor. He is handsome, if that's important. He says he loves me.

"All Visitors Ashore!" came the stern command over the loudspeakers, repeated for the third time. "Final Notice. All Ashore That's Going Ashore", and at last the excited crowd began to move to the gangways leading to the wharf below. Last hugs, tears, promises to write--no, I won't forget, have a good time, say hello to the Pope when you get to Rome, don't forget to ring Uncle Arthur when you're in London, don't do anything I wouldn't do! HaHa! Give the Queen my love, be safe, love you, love, kisses, hugs, hurry up or we'll be stowaways.

Running to the rail, Thalia groped in her raincoat pocket for the red bandanna and the rolls of streamers that her family had given her, with instructions: “When you see us on the wharf, wave the red hankie so we can pick you out, then throw a streamer as hard as you can so we can catch it and hold onto it.” Everyone here has a red hankie, she thought, they'll never pick me out.

Her last conversation with her mother came back to her: “Mum! He'll be there in Vancouver, I know he will. I trust him completely. You don't know him, you think I'm stupid and silly, but I'm not. I'm 25 years old, an adult. It's going to be all right, you'll see.”

“Well, that's just lovely, missy, but what if he's not there? How will you get home again? Why didn't he come back to Australia to get married? Why are you getting married in Canada? And you're leaving the Church--why?”

“Which question do you want me to answer first? If he's not there, I don't know. I can find a job in Canada, work for a while to earn enough money to come home. I've never had a problem getting a job before. But he will be there. And he didn't come back because we couldn't afford the fares--round trip across the Pacific for him, plus a single for me isn't cheap, you know. And we need to get married before we can apply for an immigrant visa for me, that's why.”

“And what about your faith? Why leave the Church?”

“Because he’s not a Catholic and we don’t want a mixed marriage! And anyway, neither of us believes that stuff any more. It’s 1965, the world’s changing, the war’s really over, and long past. Life’s better for us all, and besides--admit that you don’t believe in religion either. Be honest, at least.”

As her mother's voice faded from her mind, she could see her people down below, all together--young brother James wearing one of his fancy Italian sweaters, Mum, waving wildly to catch Thalia’s attention. And, hanging back a bit, not entirely comfortable with the emotion of the occasion, her lifelong friend Pam, Rose Red to Thalia’s Snow White, beloved confidante, partner in mischief, annoyance to nuns, competitor sometimes, but always there.

Pam, practical to the soles of her feet and tips of her fingers, had asked her the other day, "Tally, why? Is it some romantic idea of sailing on the midnight tide, meeting your lover in a faraway country, being the mysterious foreigner--a kind of wistful daydream?” Thalia hadn't answered, just smiled dreamily and turned away, as Pam, exasperated, said, "Oh, you were such a bookworm when we were kids, I think you read too much. Come down to earth."

Throwing the paper streamers one after the other--white, yellow, green, blue, pink, watching some of them caught by strangers, but others successfully connecting her with those she loved--diverted Thalia for a few minutes. The gangways were up now, the heavy ropes holding the ship against the land were cast off, and *Oriana* began to move majestically from the wharf as the band began to play the "Maori Farewell" and the crowd joined in singing the well-loved words:

Now is the hour
When we must say goodbye
Soon you'll be sailing far across the sea
While you're away,
Oh, please remember me

The streamers grew taut, Thalia reached out to give them more play, but as the ship moved from the quay, they snapped--the slender paper streamers seeming to symbolize the umbilical nourishments of mother, family, duty, and country broke under the strain and Thalia began to cry. She was alone. She felt nervous tension, sadness, uncertainty, but also hope and yearning and the youthful need for her own experiences, her own decisions, even her own mistakes.

Oriana pulled away at midnight; led by the harbor pilot, she swung her bow to face the outbound channel. The band played "Waltzing Matilda", the faces on the wharf diminished until they were dots, unrecognizable, as the tugs led the great ship under the Harbor Bridge, down Port Jackson past the warships at Garden Island, past Bennelong Point and Rose Bay, and safely out into deep water. The ferries, familiar to Thalia as prosaic everyday transportation, flashed like scarabs in the darkness as they stood away from the procession of tugs and liner.

As the ship sailed out between the rocky headlands which mark Port Jackson's exit to the ocean, the harbor pilot was dropped off and the ship's band packed up their instruments while the crew cleaned up the torn streamers. The lights on the decks were extinguished as they left the land behind. It's dark out there on the Pacific Ocean when the land falls away. But for the ship's navigation lights, there is no light except what comes from the moon and stars, and there are no sounds but the throb of the engines and the susurration of the ship's progress through the dark water. You have fallen into a void, and even with the confidence and ignorance of twenty-five, it was hard for Thalia not to feel some doubt about what she was doing.

Her fiancé Douglas, the American man she had met a year ago in Melbourne, had written and proposed marriage after his return to the US. Would he really be waiting for her in Vancouver? Her mother's voice came back to her. What if her mother was right? She could still turn back at Auckland, face the embarrassment, settle for the known and safe, obey the Church and her family like a good Catholic girl. Should she? Suddenly chilled, she turned and went below to find her cabin.

Chapter Two
The Albatross

As she had expected, the cabin was spartan. And tiny. Two bunks, an upper and a lower, with her luggage on the lower one and no indication of any other occupant, implying that perhaps she would have it to herself at least until Auckland. A single chair and two small dressers provided the remainder of the furniture; the floor was linoleum, and there was no bathroom, just a washbasin in the corner. Presumably the bathroom was down the hall--she corrected herself mentally--the gangway. But the cabin was hers alone, at least for the next few days.

She kept hearing her mother's voice in her head. "Thalia, are you sure? Maybe you could talk to Father O'Brien one more time? You were such a devout little girl, I always thought you would be a nun, but..." Now that the emotion of parting was over, she could hear more clearly the love and concern in it. Her mother, like all Thalia's family, had very little use for the outward expression of feelings. Shaped by hard times and personal misfortune, they were practical people, Irish Catholic, "lace curtain Irish", who put a high value on respectability and religion.

"Mum! I would never be a nun! That was all acting. I liked the blue cloaks the Children of Mary wore, the Latin, the incense, and it made the nuns nicer to me than they were to 'naughty' girls. Did you really think that?"

"Oh, I don't know--yes, I suppose I did. What about talking to Sister Mary Rita? You always liked her, and maybe she can convince you..."

"I am not going to talk to anyone else. I've listened to everyone, and it won't make any difference. You all have to stop this--Auntie Sheila, Gran, everybody. Every time I answer the phone, it's someone else. The pope hasn't rung me up yet. I wonder why not?"

The voices went on and on in her head. Mother, aunts, priest, even her young brother, although his voice was more sympathetic. "Tally, I think I understand, It's hard to get away from family round here. But we--well I--will miss you a lot." Tired now, worn out by the roller coaster of emotions, Thalia moved the luggage off the bunk and lay down, pulling the cotton bedspread over her and hoping to sleep. When she turned out the light, the tiny room was as black as the inside of your pocket. There was no window, no porthole, nothing to indicate that there was a windy world four decks above. Suddenly, she craved fresh air and the dark sea with its limitless expanse; turning the light back on, she jumped up and ran out of the room, slamming the door behind her and heading up the stairs toward the open deck.

.

Thalia had travelled by sea on several of the ships that served the coastal capitals of Australia, and had learned to enjoy the creaking of the vessel as it flexed and rolled with the motion of the waves. Tonight there was little movement; the sea seemed very calm, or perhaps the highly-publicized modern stabilizing equipment of this P&O liner was in use. When she reached the open deck, she turned aft and saw in front of her a wide curved space, open to the sky. As she came closer, she realized that it was a dimly-lit outdoor lounge overlooking the stern. She stood at the rail, fascinated by the turbulent white wake that followed the ship. There was no moon, but the Magellanic Cloud, blazing along the Milky Way, provided a mysterious and shadowless light to which her eyes accustomed themselves quickly.

Suddenly, something swooped low across the water, then rose into the darkness and vanished, but seconds later, it returned on a downward arc across the wake and again, disappeared. Thalia watched and again--swoop, vanish, return. A voice from one of the chairs nearby said, "It's a wandering albatross. They follow the ships in this hemisphere, sometimes for weeks. This one just picked us up an hour or so ago. Sorry if I startled you. I thought you might want to know."

Turning toward the voice, she said, "Yes, you made me jump a bit. I had no idea there was anyone here but me!" Now she could see his outline, and the glow of a cigarette. "I did know about the albatross but thanks. I've seen them other times in the Southern Ocean, and I always find them thrilling."

The male voice, British and cultured although slightly raspy--perhaps a smoker, she thought--replied "Oh, you've travelled down in this part of the world before, then? Are you a tourist or a traveller?"

Puzzled, Thalia asked, "What's the difference? I don't understand."

"A tourist is a sightseer. A traveller is someone who has a purpose for the journey--work, a move, family matters. I'm a traveller--I've been working in Australia for a year, and it's time to go home to London. You?"

"Oh. A traveller. Well, maybe a bit of both, because it's my first time out of Australia. But what do you do that brought you to Australia for so long?" asked Thalia, then catching something theatrical in the voice--timbre, accent, careful delivery? "No, wait! Let me guess...you're an actor."

"Good guess! Yes, I've been playing theatres in Melbourne and Sydney but the play has finished its run and I'm tired. A couple of weeks of shipboard relaxation on the way home. My name's Nigel Somerville."

"How do you do?" said Thalia, "I'm Thalia McGrath, from Melbourne, and I am on my way to Vancouver to get married." She realized that it was beginning to get light, the stars were fading and now she could see the arc of the albatross's flight--wide figure eights across the wake, with a low swoop across the water each time. "Do you think the bird is feeding from the water down there?"

Nigel answered slowly, "Perhaps. They're pelagic--I looked them up. Sometimes they stay at sea for months, so I suppose they must feed somehow: small fish, plankton, microscopic creatures. I don't know. There's an encyclopedia in the library, we could look it up some more." He stood up, and there was enough light for Thalia to see him for the first time. Tall, about her own age she thought, with dark hair well-cut but a little longer than usually worn by Australian or American men, he moved gracefully, displaying none of the awkwardness often shown by tall, longboned men. Laughing, he said "I don't suppose they have much of a domestic life, spending so much time at sea. Perhaps they have seagoing affairs, casual meetings, no obligations--like shipboard romances, sweet and intense, but withering at the sight of land."

"In "The Rime of the Ancient Mariner", Coleridge says it's "the bird of good omen" for sailors." Thalia said, "In the poem, a ship had been driven into the Antarctic region of the world by a terrible wind, and the crew lost hope of rescue, but a bird, an albatross, appeared. It led the ship northward and out of the "wondrous cold", and the sailors regained hope and were grateful. But the Ancient Mariner shot it with his crossbow, and now he must carry the dead albatross and the guilt forever. Guilt for the death of hope--a crime without atonement." She shivered, then laughed, "I need a British breakfast and a bit more sleep. Thank you for the interesting conversation, and I hope we see one another again."

Giving a little wave, she turned to leave, but, "Thalia, wait!" he called "Let's make sure we do. I want to continue our talk, and get to know you better. You haven't told me about your fiancé yet. The library at eleven?"

"Alright. See you then."

A steward appeared from within, sounding a little gong and chanting, "First call for breakfast. Serving in fifteen minutes." and Thalia headed down to her cabin to unpack and change the clothes she had been wearing for the past twenty-four hours. She had made her first acquaintance on board ship; now she had someone to talk to and not feel so out-of-place. But had this little meeting moved too quickly? The ".. get to know you better" seemed a little presumptuous. Had she maybe suggested a willingness for more than friendship with her remarks? Somewhere deep inside her mind was a flare of caution, an instinctive understanding of the need for care in a new and potentially dangerous situation. She remembered Auntie Kath's stories of card sharps and thefts from her cabin that she had experienced on an earlier voyage. Thalia had mentally scoffed at the doubts and worries of an older generation, but some of it had stuck in her head. I will be careful, she thought, as she opened her cabin door.

Chapter Three

Douglas

When Thalia arrived in the dining room for breakfast, she found a line of passengers waiting to be given their table assignments for the voyage. A lively group of three young women joined the queue behind her and included her in their conversation.

"Where are you going?" inquired a pretty blonde, in a fluting British accent, "we're going all the way to home! We've been larking around Australia for a year now, and it's time we got back to work."

"I'm going as far as Vancouver." replied Thalia. "My name's Thalia McGrath, I'm Australian, and I'm on my way to a wedding."

"A wedding! How exciting!" the group said in unison, then the fluttery blonde began to introduce them. "I'm Isabelle Sanderson, and next to me is my sister Sybil. I'm the beauty of the family," laughing as her sister rolled her eyes at her, "but she doesn't know it, and the third", indicating a slim girl, her hair pulled back into a knot low on her neck, and dressed in a pullover and trousers, "is Dorrie Magnus, she's one of the horsey Magnus's. She was hoping for a rich Aussie, one of those squatters we all heard about--lots of money, keep racehorses, no women in their lives, and thirsting for the feminine touch in their outback mansions."

Sybil spoke up. "No romance for any of us, really! Our little fishing fleet is going home disappointed."

Dorrie, looking a bit wistful, said "I think we were misled. The only rich ones I met were fat and whiskery, and smelled of cigarette smoke and beer. Definitely no interest in the "feminine touch", unless it's in bed. And those awful Orstralian accents! How do you do, Thalia?"

A bit shocked by the casual mention of bed in this context, Thalia smiled and began to speak (carefully, trying to minimize her accent) but the steward at the desk asked for her name and cabin number, then said "Oh, you've already been assigned to Table 35. It's over in the corner." She looked in the direction he indicated and saw Nigel standing at the table waving to her, and turned back to the little feminine group, saying "It's been lovely meeting you all! Can we meet later today?"

Isabelle said, "Yes--I was going to suggest the bar on the pool deck. It's where everyone meets for drinks before lunch. And you know all about us now, so we want to quiz you about this wedding you're going to attend. See you at noon."

The dining room, deep amidships to minimize the effects of rough seas on the diners, was large and crowded. Stewards were busy bringing plates of food from the kitchen--full British breakfasts, Thalia noticed. Eggs, sausages, porridge, grilled tomatoes, toast in silver racks, silver pots of tea, with the smell of kippers and kedgeree floating in the air. Lucky the sea is calm today, thought Thalia, wondering how many people would be ordering kippers and kedgeree on a stormy day.

"I got you a good table assignment," Nigel said, as she arrived at the table where he stood. "I hope you don't mind. Please sit down and let me introduce you to my friends," as he pulled out an empty chair from the table for her and she sat down. "Everyone, this is Thalia, who knows all about albatrosses, and who is leaving Australia for the first time. She is apparently an insomniac like me. We met on the poop deck at 3 a.m."

A woman sitting at the other side of the table called out, "Hello, Thalia! Welcome to our little group. I'm Charmian, and this gentleman next to me is Julian. We are all from Nigel's theatre company, going home in a gaggle with the albatross. And is there really something called a 'poop deck'?" As she spoke, she turned a gold cigarette case over on the table, then took out a cigarette, leaning toward Julian and gesturing to him to light it for her. Her manner seemed brittle and a little abrupt to Thalia, although Julian complied with the request with a flourish of his lighter and a mocking smile.

Julian, an imposing man with grey hair and the profile of a Roman emperor on an ancient coin, began to speak, but before he could complete a word, the woman on the other side of Charmian said, "I don't think albatrosses fly in gaggles, Charmian. Hello, Thalia. I'm Amelia, and I'm not nearly as prim as my name suggests. I can be quite shocking if I'm in the mood." Amelia, auburn-haired and no longer young, was very thin, with blade-sharp cheekbones, brown eyes, and a theatrical, British upper-class drawl. Her hand with long painted nails held a cigarette in a green holder, and she squinted a little through the smoke that was twisting in front of her. Despite the squint, her eyes were sharp and observant.

"Thalia, ignore them," said Nigel, "they're all giddy with delight that the drinks on board are really cheap, the season is over, and they got paid. Julian speaks sometimes when he's allowed, but mostly in proclamations and only when his voice is well-lubricated with good whiskey; he's played too many senior politicians and very important people." Julian mimed a little bow, inclining his head graciously.

Beginning to feel that this voyage would not be dull, Thalia said, "I am so happy to meet you all. Tell me about your play. I come from Melbourne, but I have been in

Western Australia for the past year, so I haven't seen any current theatre lately."

"No, Thalia, we are tired of that boring play. We want to hear about you. Nigel says you are going to Canada to get married." said Charmian. "How exotic! Who are you marrying, and why are you going so far to tie the knot?"

"Not exotic really, just practical! Douglas, my fiancé, is a journalist, he was working in Australia for a couple of years, but he had to go back to Washington. We couldn't afford the additional fares across the Pacific for him to come back so we set things up this way."

Amelia asked, "How does your family feel about this? Are they happy that you won't be married at home?"

Thalia winced. "You've hit a sore point! No, they aren't happy, and they are sure he won't be there and I will be stranded in Canada without a penny, and I will come to a bad end."

"Well, you had better eat up, then," advised Julian in a rich baritone voice, "maybe famine ahead! I hope you ordered one of everything on offer, did you?" as the food arrived, and they began to eat and question Thalia about Douglas and their romance. Veterans of the London theatre, they were a close group among themselves and seemingly needed no-one else for amusement, leaving

Thalia wondering why Nigel had been so quick to bring her into the circle. Again, there was a little flash of caution in her mind.

The stewards served the food, and in answer to questions, Thalia said "Douglas and I met when he was doing a story on life in the outback, on the big sheep stations in Queensland and New South Wales. He needed some introductions to the squatters--the big farmers are called squatters--out there, and I know a few of their kids from boarding school in Melbourne, so I was able to arrange some meetings."

"I hear it's pretty rough," said Nigel, "heat, dust, sand and flies".

"Well, 'the green and shaded lanes of England' it's not," Thalia replied, "and in The Wet, it's mostly rain, mud, mutton and flies. But he had a great time and got a good story, and when he got back into town he rang me up to thank me, and asked me out to dinner. And here I am..." As they talked, she became aware that the ship was rolling more. Some people were leaving the dining room hurriedly. "Looks like we're heading into some weather, doesn't it? Thank you all for letting me join your group, and I think I'll go on deck now."

Nigel followed her as she left the dining salon, and caught up to her on the stairs to the upper deck. "I hope they didn't intimidate you too much, Thalia. They really are good people, not nasty or mean, but they sometimes forget that other people aren't accustomed to their theatricality, their inside jokes, and so on."

"No, they're interesting, and I look forward to hearing some of the stories of theatre life. It seems really different from my suburban existence." They emerged from the stairway onto the promenade deck, a windowed space protected from the weather by glass panes washed by water from waves and rain. "The weather has really changed, hasn't it? We're in the Tasman Sea, and it's notorious for sudden storminess." Thalia said.

"If we go aft, we can probably see the wake from under cover, and see if the albatross is still with us. Thalia, I would really like to know more about you. Perhaps we can get to know one another well on the voyage, and part as real friends."

"Well, let's wait and see! Now I think I will go to the library. I need to write some letters to mail in New Zealand. I promised Douglas that I would write every day."

Chapter Four

A Storm in the Tasman Sea

Thalia realized that the ship was rolling hard now, and that the waves were growing larger, with spray blowing off their crests and veins of white froth mottling their dark surface. The wind and spray were sweeping across the exposed deck, and passengers were leaving quickly to seek shelter inside.

The albatross was still accompanying the ship, flying easily and sometimes dipping the tip of a wing into the waves. The long narrow wings, edged and tipped with black, moved smoothly as the bird adjusted its course. Against the measureless background of the ocean, it was almost impossible to gauge their span; Thalia had read that they could measure up to 11 feet, making the wandering albatross of the Southern Ocean the largest of flying birds. Beautiful in flight, with a romantically solitary way of life, what had led a nineteenth-century English poet to choose this creature as a symbol of the death of hope, she wondered?

"Nigel, I'm going inside now." Thalia said, shouting a little because the wind was beginning to howl. "Thanks for including me at your table. I'm sure I'll enjoy the group. See you at lunch!" She was beginning to feel uncomfortable with Nigel's attentions. Was he a bit too eager? As she left the deck, Nigel began to follow her but stopped as Julian appeared nearby; Thalia made her way to the library.

Such a beautiful room, she thought, with dark woodwork, deep carpeting and high shelves filled with richly-bound books, including the volumes of Encyclopedia Britannica, and a sturdy antique stand holding a large dictionary. Only a few people were inside, some reading in the big comfortable leather chairs, others using the writing desks and the P&O stationery. She settled at a desk, and began a letter to Douglas that she intended to mail in New Zealand... "*Dearest Douglas, On the way at last! Only two short weeks until we will be together to begin our new lives! I am...*" Suddenly, she stopped writing. I am... what? I don't know. Am I excited? Am I scared? Am I in love with Douglas? Have I made a huge mistake? Is my family right? Questions questions questions, no answers only questions. What on earth can I say in a letter?

As Thalia sat pondering this, and for the first time understanding that her twenty-five years of age did not necessarily bestow much wisdom, Amelia arrived. Amelia, she of the sultry chuckle, the green quartz cigarette holder, and the self-implied naughtiness of character. "Hello, Thalia," she purred throatily, "how nice to find a friend here. Everyone else seems to be suffering from a touch of *mal de mer*. You don't suffer from it?"

"No. I never have. I used to sail with my father, and he always loved rough water and a challenge. If I wanted to be on board, I couldn't get seasick or I would be left on shore. And rough water in the Tasman Sea is pretty routine. It has a reputation for sudden violent storms, but they generally pass quickly, and by dinnertime it will probably all be over."

"Good to know. But for now, the bar's open, I can't smoke in this room, and they say rum is a great little preventer of *mal de mer.* Will you join me over a dram?" Thalia blinked. Rum so early in the day? She certainly wasn't in staid Melbourne any more, she thought.

"Well, the bar would be fine. I'm not too sure about rum in the morning, but if they will let me have coffee, I'm in."

"Brava, little Thalia! Let's go and meet the bartenders." And Amelia led the way down the gangway to the enclosed bar, where they were greeted with cheers from the bartenders who were supervising empty tables while the waves threw dollops of salt water against the windows and the howl of the wind increased.

They chose a table next to a streaming window, and gave their orders to the handsome young steward who greeted them with, "Survivors! Captain says this will get worse before it gets better, so drink up. If it gets too bad, we have to shut down but with a load of Aussies on board, that's a really unpopular thing to do; they want their beer."

Amelia pulled out a cigarette and the green holder. Quickly the steward was there with a lighter, Amelia steadying his hand with hers for an instant as she lit the cigarette and inhaled, then giving him a murmured thank you and a sideways glance from under her long eyelashes. False lashes, Thalia wondered, as she watched this tiny performance with fascination; the young man stood there for a little too long before withdrawing his lighter and returning to the bar. Amelia said "Possibilities there, I think, for amusement ahead. What do you think, Thalia?"

Thalia, at sea in more ways than on board ship, said "Ummm, perhaps. I don't know what to say." Then, not wanting to seem naive, "I suppose it depends on what you are looking for."

Laughing, Amelia said, "what do you think I am looking for, Thalia? What could I possibly want from that boy?" Then she asked, "Thalia, are you a virgin?"

"I don't think I want to answer that, Amelia." No-one had ever asked Thalia that before. Why would they? To her family and friends, she was a good Catholic girl, and Catholic girls are supposed to have no interest in such things as sex before marriage. Or perhaps after marriage either, really, Thalia thought. Although, she did admit, privately and to herself alone, that she was curious. Was it as wonderful as the magazine stories made out?

"Oh," said Amelia, with a little feline smile, "I see the answer's yes. Well, perhaps this trip's a good time to practice a little." Amid her confusion, Thalia realized that Amelia was playing with her like a cat with a mouse, enjoying her discomfort. "I think you could find some willing partners along the way. Douglas might appreciate a tiny bit of experience, you know."

"There you are! I have been looking everywhere for you two!" Julian's baritone voice echoed around the empty bar, and Thalia was saved from continuing the conversation with Amelia. He stopped at the bar for a moment to order a drink, and seeing the direction of Thalia's glance, Amelia said slyly, "He's not your sort. Different tastes, if you know what I mean. Nigel's a better bet...", cutting off her sentence as Julian approached the table.

Thalia, grateful for his sudden appearance, thought again of a Roman emperor--tall, bulky although not fat, dignity personified, she could almost see the purple robe and the laurel wreath. "Nigel said you were going to the library, Thalia, but you weren't there, and the cute library steward said you had left with an older woman. I couldn't imagine who until I saw Amelia here. Got a ciggie, Amelia love?"

Suddenly the focus changed; now she saw an aging man, handsome and slightly effeminate, trying to hold onto youth and fortune in a changing world.

"Smoking's bad for you, Julian," Amelia said, as the smoke from her own cigarette wreathed around her, "bad for your boyish looks and charm. You really should stop or buy your own and stop cadging mine." She pushed the little package across the table to him and said, "Thalia was just asking about the theatrical life. You've been in it a lot longer than I have, so why don't *you* tell her about it."

"What do you want to know, Thalia?" he asked. "Glamour, excitement, London opening nights, royals in the middle box, tiaras and white fox furs, flowers, long white kid gloves, and handsome leading men? Or provincial rep, six nights and two matinees a week, potboiler plays, bedsitters in unheated old houses, boarding house food, for a pittance?" Julian paused, laughed sourly, and said, "I mean--do you want the Australian Women's Weekly version, or the truth? Truth often has a way of being unpalatable when it refuses to conform to our wishes."

Before Thalia could answer, the ship thudded down hard, then reared up. She said "Oh, the ship's starting to pitch. That's horrid." as it thudded again.

Amelia grimaced, "I hope it doesn't last too long or there won't be many passengers out of their cabins, including me."

"I wonder if the albatross is still with us, or has this storm driven it away? I think I will go and look." said Thalia as she escaped, although still asking herself questions. What is truth? Am I too naive? And is Amelia right about experience?

Chapter Five
Peril on the Sea

The storm increased throughout the day, and lunch and dinner were sparsely attended, most passengers preferring to remain in their cabins. There were ropes slung around the gangways to give passengers handholds to help them move around safely, although not many people were about. In the dining room, the tablecloths had been dampened to keep plates and utensils from sliding around as the ship rolled in heavy seas. Thalia, the only member of Table 35's group to appear at dinner, found herself at a different table, with two elderly women and three empty chairs.

An air of unease pervaded the little group. The two ladies, British as bedsocks and hot water bottles, were determined to be courageous. The elder, Mrs. Violet Framingham, said "We must carry on!" as she related to Thalia stories of the courage of Londoners during the Blitz, and her sister, Mrs. Poppy Carruthers, spoke of shipwrecks and the need for bravery and endurance. Thalia, who had been quite enjoying the drama and excitement of the storm, decided to go to bed before she was expected to join in a chorus of "For Those in Peril on the Sea".

By morning, *Oriana* had left the storm behind, and the sea had calmed considerably. The sun was shining, the water was blue, and the morning shuffleboard players were in action as Thalia came on deck. She was planning to take coffee and toast from the bar to a table near the stern where she could watch the albatross and clear her mind of the questions which seemed to be piling up there. She had not yet completed the letter to Matthew. Two more days until the ship would dock in Auckland and mail go ashore.

The great bird was still there, soaring above the tumultuous water of the ship's wake, its breast feathers pristine white, its wings making minute barely-visible adjustments to its course. Thalia watched for a while, enjoying the view and the airy, windy silence. Suddenly, one of the English girls slid into the chair next to her and said, "Here you are! We have been wondering where you went yesterday. What is that bird doing?"

"Oh, hello. It's riding the wind." said Thalia. "Let me see--you're Isabelle. Is that right?"

"Brilliant! Yes, I'm the chatterer. The others are not out of bed yet. They didn't have a very good day yesterday. Who is that toothsome chap who called you over to a table in the dining room?"

"That's Nigel. He's an actor, going back to England with a group of other actors after playing in Australia for a year."

"I think I would like to meet him! What are the others like?"

"Do you always end with a question? Why don't you see for yourself? They'll show up pretty soon, I think, for their morning refreshment. They'll join us here."

As she said that, Julian appeared at her side. Wearing a silk shirt and cravat, he was magisterial and dignified, and Thalia almost expected to hear a flourish of trumpets announcing his arrival. "So, little Thalia, where have you been? And who is this pretty thing sitting next to you?" As Thalia introduced Isabelle, Charmian and Amelia arrived together, both wearing fashionable sundresses and sandals, and sat down at the table in a little commotion of chair moving and introductions. They both pulled out cigarette cases, and Amelia looked around for the attentive steward. Julian continued, "and now we're all here, all but Nigel, the baby of our group, and I see him coming now."

Nigel arrived, standing behind Thalia's chair, and putting a hand on her shoulder as he said "Good morning, everyone." Thalia reddened, and her embarrassment at the touch was apparent to everyone at the table; Amelia and Charmian looked away, while Isabelle's eyes widened.

Julian said, "Sit down, Nigel, and leave Thalia alone. What does everyone want to drink, it's my shout this morning. The steward's on the way over, so give him your orders." Nigel sat down in a chair on the edge of the group, crossed his legs, lit a cigarette, and sulked.

Amelia said, "I have news! I found out who is number six at our table, people."

"How did you find that out?" asked Charmian, "do you have a special source?"

The handsome young steward of yesterday arrived to take their orders, and Thalia realized that Amelia's cabin number had been on the drinks bill yesterday, and that she did indeed have a special source, "and who is it? It can't be a passenger, unless they're coming aboard in Auckland."

"No, no--someone who's already here. And there he is, over there, talking to those two old ladies."

Isabelle said, "Those are Violet and Poppy, and they are our tablemates, Lord save us all! I was sent up here this morning to talk to the purser and get a new table assignment for us."

"Well, this will save you going to the purser's office, dear," from Charmian, "that's the purser himself. Aren't we lucky? And isn't he dishy in his uniform?"

Thalia, still smarting a little from Nigel's proprietorial touch on her shoulder, said, "Yes, he is! He looks nice too, not just handsome...and the purser's a very useful person to know."

Amelia snickered. "Well, if that's all that matters to you, Thalia, but remember my advice from yesterday."

Charmian, who had been smoking quietly, said suddenly, "Amelia, stop teasing Thalia" and Thalia, grateful for the support, suddenly felt Charmian might be an ally if there were battles to be fought on this voyage. The shuffleboard players had finished their match and were flocking into the bar now; it was noisy and sociable, as people began to relax and make new friends over drinks.

The purser made his way to their group, and said, "Well! Looks like you have to put up with being at my table in the dining room. Could be better, could be worse, but I don't think you'll suffer from being with me. My name is David Springer, I'm the purser of the *Oriana*, and now, I would like to meet you all. You have to tolerate me for the next however many days!"

He turned his attention to Isabelle, who said, "I am supposed to ask you to reassign me and my two friends to another table. We are presently at a table with...".

"Ah, yes, Violet and Poppy. I was just talking to them. Lovely ladies, both of them, but perhaps not quite your style. Let's see what I can do. There's a table for ten that is not in use yet--would you like to join me and this group there?"

"Do you need to ask? I will tell the others. We are ever so grateful!"

"That's what I'm here for, to be helpful to our passengers, to make the journey pleasant for them. Our crew takes its responsibilities seriously." he said, as the young steward bent down to light the cigarette Amelia offered him, and Charmian gave Thalia a knowing look. On the edge of the group, Nigel sulked ostentatiously, ignoring everyone.

Thalia watched David Springer as he spoke to each member of the group, giving each of them his full attention, enfolding them gently in a net of charm and kindness. He isn't really handsome, she thought, not in the conventional sense, but he is attractive--dark eyes, curly black hair, tanned skin, and a smile that brought the sun. Suddenly, she thought--sex appeal, that's what it is! I've never felt it before, not really. As her turn came, she found herself tonguetied and stammering. "You must be Thalia McGrath," he said, "I saw the list of my tablemates, and you are the only one not with the theatre group. You're going to Vancouver, I understand."

"Yes."

Patiently, he asked, "What are you planning to do in Canada?" Thalia gulped, then scrambled for an answer.

"I... think I am going to get married." What is happening to me, she thought. "... 'I *think*?' I think I have been hit by lightning, that's what I think. I am dying to say "I want you! I want to go to bed with you, David Springer."

The steward with the gong passed by, sounding out his little mealtime summons. Lunch was served and they trooped down to the dining room, leaving Isabelle to wait for her companions. The table was re-seated by the purser, who placed Thalia to his right, and Charmian to his left. The stormy weather was gone, and there was no current peril on the sea, meteorologically at least.

Amelia, cigarette and lighter at the ready, gold bangle dangling on her wrist, sat down at the table, chuckled and looked at Julian, who said, "I think Thalia is about to get some interesting experience." Nigel said nothing.

Chapter Six
David Springer

Dinner was festive that evening; tomorrow *Oriana* would dock in Auckland, some passengers would depart and others embark, and then the ship would begin the longest part of its journey, across Polynesia to Fiji and then to Hawai'i.

The little group of English girls joined the table en masse for the first time, providing an amusing distraction with their chatter about being a husband-fishing fleet to the Commonwealth. Thalia was disappointed that David Springer failed to show up; he sent a message to the table that he was needed in his office for a while, but would be there as soon as possible. "How disappointing," Amelia said, then turning to Thalia "you look very pretty tonight. Are you dressed for someone special?"

Thalia, wary of Amelia, answered briefly. "Not really, I just unpacked a little more today so I would have something different to wear," although Amelia's comment was uncomfortably close to the truth, and she had chosen the strapless cotton frock because of its flattering color, swinging skirt, and how it showed off her tiny waist.

Isabelle asked Julian to tell her about life in the theatrical world. "I mean... I *LOVE* the theatre and Mummy always takes us to the pantomime, and it all seems so glam... ". Julian, flattered by the attention of three pretty, lively, and possibly rich young women, expanded like a Japanese paper flower dropped in water and began to reminisce...

"It was an emotional scene--the end of a marriage. The hero's departure, leaving the unfaithful wife *forever*! I marched to the door to fling it open and exit in a grand dramatic gesture and... the doorknob came off in my hand."

"Oh, no. What did you do?" asked Dorrie.

"I flung the doorknob across the stage--just missed the stage manager standing in the wings--and shouted, 'and I will never enter this ramshackle hovel again', then jumped through the window," Julian said, "the audience loved it. Stage manager wasn't so keen though."

His audience--Dorrie, Isabelle and the others of what Thalia thought of now as The Fleet--was entranced. Amelia laughed and said "Well, you didn't really JUMP. You sort of fell through the window and wrecked it! The stage manager said you pulled the knob too hard, and it left me stuck on stage by myself. Nigel, my lover, was supposed to rush in through the same door and console me, but it wouldn't open from offstage either. I had to sit sobbing and crying all by myself for five minutes while they tried to pry it open."

Nigel, recovered from his sulk but not looking at Thalia, said, "Well, you always do like to have the limelight to yourself, Amelia. You made the most of it, didn't you?"

"Yes, she did." Charmian said, nodding agreement, "Mopping tears with that silly chiffon hankie, flashing that BIG fake diamond in the lights--attention grabbing! You could have adlibbed something helpful instead."

"Like what? And why? I was having a wonderful time." answered Amelia, "oh, look, here's *our* hero now. Smile, Thalia."

David Springer was making his way toward the table, threading through the room greeting people. He slipped into his chair and introduced himself to Dorrie and Sybil, who were at the table for the first time, and said, "we will have another passenger at the table tomorrow night. When we leave Auckland, a new traveler will join us and the table will be complete."

The group at the table began to relax and get to know one another; the conversation was lively, theatrical anecdotes mixing with the girls' stories of their adventures Down Under, Dorrie repeating her comments about the lack of attractive, rich horsemen. Suddenly she said, "Thalia, I just realized that I have met your Douglas! I was staying on my cousin's cattle station for a few days and an American journalist visited there! We went riding together, and he was lovely--you're so lucky!"

Thalia asked her cousin's name, and said, "Oh, yes! She's Pam's friend. Pam's my oldest friend in the world. She and your cousin met when they were at boarding school together, and Pam put Douglas in touch with her. What a small world this is... "

Thalia began to notice a warm pressure against her leg. David's leg was bumping hers from time to time, and seemed to be remaining there a little longer each time. He continued to talk to everyone at the table, not paying special attention to her apparently, except that his leg was now staying put against hers. Am I reading something into this that isn't there, Thalia asked herself? Surely it's accidental. He dropped his serviette, which fell to the floor and, as he dived to retrieve it, she felt his hand brush her thigh gently and leave behind a slip of paper.

Well, she thought, not accidental and he certainly has my attention now. How can I read it? I can't just fish it out in front of all these people. Wouldn't Amelia love that? Thalia used her serviette to blot her lips, then laid it back in her lap, covering her left hand. With that hand, she carefully retrieved the note, palmed it, then opened her little evening bag lying on the table to search for a handkerchief. There. The note was safely inside.

Dinner passed excruciatingly slowly for Thalia. At last, she excused herself, saying she had to finish her letter to Douglas and get it to the purser's office so it could go in the morning's mail, and made her way up to the library, where she extracted the note from her evening bag and laid it on the desk. Nigel appeared suddenly and flung himself into a nearby chair, saying, "why are you avoiding me, Thalia?"

Hastily covering the note with a sheet of writing paper, Thalia sighed and said, "I'm not avoiding you, Nigel. Can't we just be friends and not have drama and tension, please?"

"Well, come and have coffee with me now, then. Let's see if the albatross is still there."

"Let me write my letter, then I'll meet you in the bar before the dance. Alright?"

"Jolly good! See you then. And by the by, don't let Amelia upset you. She's a legendary harpy. Just be careful though, because she can be dangerous if you cross her."

Her head full of confused emotions and curiosity about the contents of the note, she dutifully wrote her letter to

Douglas before reading it: "*Dearest Douglas, so much to tell you, so many things happening around me, all very exciting! Meeting new people all the time, enjoying shipboard life, but SO much looking forward to seeing you in Vancouver, and beginning our new life together. Hastily, trying to get this in the morning's post, All my love, Thalia*". And that will have to do for tonight, she thought.

Then, still sitting at the writing desk, she unfolded David's note. Just a slip of notebook paper torn at the edges, it said, "*Thalia, I believe you felt it too, the lightning flash? Please meet me at midnight tomorrow in the stern lounge.*"

Putting Douglas's letter in her bag, she left the library with David's note crumpled in her hand. As she emerged onto the rear deck and arrived at the rail, she could see that the albatross was still gliding above the ship's wake, and realized that the air was warmer than it had been earlier in the day. We're entering the tropics now, she thought, on the edge of the great triangle of Polynesia which cuts across the Pacific from New Zealand in the west to Easter Island in the east with Hawai'i its northerly apex. This is my first time leaving Australia. Do I want to mark that milestone by becoming involved with a man who thinks that playing kneesie under the table is a good way to get to know a woman? And about whom I know nothing except that he has stirred strong feelings in me?

Carefully, she tore the note into tiny pieces and, leaning over the rail with the wind behind her, let the fragments spill from her hand into the air where they whirled in a miniature snowstorm for a moment before dropping into the ocean and disappearing. The albatross paid no attention, gliding back and forth like a feathered metronome.

Chapter Seven

Thalia Wakes Up

The following evening, Thalia considered her next move. It wouldn't be smart to offend the purser, dependent as she and the others were on his goodwill during the voyage, but she had no intention of meeting him at midnight, tonight or any night. Nigel had rather neatly trumped David's hand last night anyway, she thought.

“Thalia, are you alright?” a voice behind her asked. She turned to find Dorrie looking at her with concern. “You look upset, and I could see the purser seemed to be overwhelming you a bit at dinner last night. I think he's a touch too fond of himself, that man, and a bit of a wolf, too. Do you agree?"

"Yes, I think I do! He's very practiced, isn't he?" Thalia's laugh was shaky. "I suppose he has lots of opportunity, meeting people all the time, so handsome in his uniform, all those brass buttons, and such smooth manners. I wonder if he's married?"

"Probably. But I wouldn't want to be his wife. Stuck with two kids in a suburban semi-detached in freezing England, while he swans around the South Pacific charming single women."

"He has two kids?"

"Oh, I don't know," laughing at Thalia's innocence, "but could be, couldn't it? Anyway, I thought he was trying to get close to you yesterday at the table."

The light was fading now, the rim of the sea seeming to rise and fall gently with the smooth rolling of the ship. Thinking to divert Dorrie, perhaps mislead her and provide cover for her own feelings, Thalia didn't respond to the comment and said, "Exciting that we'll be in New Zealand tomorrow! It's my first foreign country, although it's not very foreign at all! Must seem strange to you, Dorrie, England's so close to Europe, you can cross borders any time. We must seem very provincial."

"Well, most of what *I've* seen anywhere has been connected with horses. My father breeds them, and my family's horse-crazy! And New Zealand's famous for its horses--Australia's famous Phar Lap was a New Zealander, I'm sure you know that! I'm hoping to visit a stud farm outside Auckland while we're there."

"Sound more interesting than my day is going to be--meeting family, probably getting lectured again about marrying outside the church, leaving Australia, and so on. Makes me want to do something really shocking: swim naked in the pool at midnight, get drunk on champagne (I've never tasted champagne, imagine!)

have an affair!" Suddenly Thalia realized that David was offering exactly that. An affair. And also what Amelia had suggested. Experience. But maybe no champagne.

Laughing, she took Dorrie's hand and said, "Let's go to the dance! Maybe you'll meet a handsome New Zealand horseman to take home as a trophy from your big trip!"

"Wouldn't that be a joke? After all those beery, ciggie-smelling Aussies! Sorry, Thalia—don't mean to hurt your feelings, but I've met a lot of no-hopers on this trip. Let's go dancing!"

As Thalia and Dorrie opened the doors into the hallway leading to the ballroom, the sound of music poured out and reached Nigel where he was sitting unnoticed by the girls in one of the large chairs sheltered from their view by a lifeboat. He lit a cigarette and sat thoughtfully for a few minutes, watching the albatross as it passed in and out of the beam of the navigation lights, then as if making a decision, he rapidly extinguished the cigarette and followed them.

Down in the ballroom, the Mexican Hat Dance was in progress and Dorrie and Thalia were immediately swept into it by two young officers. Amelia, Charmian and Julian, seated at a cabaret table, smiled superior smiles at the sweaty young faces of the dancers on the floor as they spun, stamped, clapped hands, and circled rapidly around the gaudy Mexican hats laid on the polished floor. “Olé!” shouted the watchers, full skirts and petticoats flared out as girls were swung by partners, the stewards clicked castanets, the trumpets blared, and the drums pounded. In a final grand confusion of circling dancers, streamers were thrown across the floor and the breathless dancers collapsed into chairs, fanning themselves and laughing at being young and carefree and brave, voyaging so far away from home.

Isabelle and Sybil arrived, still panting slightly, and flopped into chairs. “Can we get a drink?” asked Isabelle of the table at large. “Are the drinks free tonight? I hope so, I’m dryzabone I just learned that bit of Aussie slang! Where’s Thalia? I saw that dishy David Springer on his way here, and I think she’s fancying him a bit, don’t you? Oh, here she is.”

Thalia sat down and said sharply, “I heard that, Isabelle! Mind your own business and leave me alone. You’re being rude.”

Julian drawled into the silence following this remark “Well, Lady Manners, why don’t we leave these ignoramii and dance? The band’s going to start up again,” as he rose imperiously from his seat, took Thalia’s hand and guided her onto the empty dance floor. The musicians, taking their cue from his gravity, began to play the Tennessee Waltz and Julian, with ponderous dignity and grace, guided Thalia around the floor. “I love a waltz,” he said, “don’t you, Thalia? So soothing, so gentle and old-fashioned, helps to heal the soul. Don’t be bothered by the others, they’re mostly jealous of you, you know. Amelia is positively green, and the English dollies too. Rise above, be a villain and get even!”

Just then, the band cut off the waltz to play a fanfare, as David Springer walked into the room and, elegant in his white tropical dress uniform, took the microphone. Oh, my, Thalia thought. He's the highwayman in the poem!

> *He’d a French cocked-hat on his forehead, a bunch of lace at his chin,*
> *A coat of the claret velvet, and breeches of brown doe-skin.*
> *They fitted with never a wrinkle. His boots were up to the thigh.*
> *And he rode with a jewelled twinkle,*
> *His pistol butts a-twinkle,*
> *His rapier hilt a-twinkle, under the jewelled sky.*

No bunch of lace at his chin of course, just a neat black bow tie, but the effect was the same--the dandyish clothes, the confident swagger, the preening of the dominant male. “Ladies and gentlemen,” he intoned genially, “I’m David Springer, purser, and this is my first opportunity to welcome you all aboard, plus my chance to say goodbye to those who are leaving us in Auckland.”

She and Julian began to return to the table as his remarks continued, Julian saying "You know, Thalia, he is really handsome, isn't he? I find him quite a temptation myself, but I know you saw him first."

Thalia laughed a little ruefully, agreeing and saying, "Oh, don't you tease me too, Julian! You managed to smooth things over for me, let's leave it now." As they arrived at the table, David reached his conclusion and asked the band to play again. The audience, rested now, began to dance to the loud strong beat of "Rock Around The Clock", the current Top of the Hit Parade. The band segued into "Shake, Shake, Señora" as a conga line formed and the dancers, chanting and laughing, conga-ed out of the ballroom, led by Julian and Thalia. Even Charmian and Amelia joined in, and Nigel was scooped up at the tail end as the line wound its way around the stern lounge and back into the ballroom from the other side. The crowd cheered and applauded as the band downed instruments and headed for the bar, Table 35's members reassembled at the cabaret table and rested, shipboard friends now, comfortable together and prepared to support their group. Amelia pulled out her cigarettes and cigarette holder, and the young steward arrived to light the offered cigarette. "A round of drinks for the table! Put the drinks on my bill," she murmured through the coiling smoke, with a sultry smile for the steward from under the false eyelashes.

The steward assented but didn't ask for her cabin number. "Well," said Charmian "I suppose he knows it," with a sidelong glance at Isabelle and Sybil, "he must have delivered something to her already."

The purser didn't show up. "Too bad, Thalia," said Amelia, "you'll have to wait to get started on your practice." It was late, they were tired, and arrival would be early next morning. One by one, they drifted off to bed. *He did not come in the dawning. He did not come at noon…*

Chapter Eight

Nigel's Proposal

David Springer stood at the rail where Thalia had stood to throw the pieces of his note to her over the side. He smiled when he saw her but made no move to speak to her. She gave a wave but continued to walk toward the stairs leading to her cabin.

Seeing her about to disappear, "Thalia, over here," called David, "I was hoping you would come," he added, walking towards her as she hesitated, reluctant to seem rude but not approaching him. Lowering his voice, he said, "Please stay; let's get to know one another. I know you felt that bolt of lightning yesterday, I could see it on your face."

Suddenly Nigel appeared on the deck, saying, "Thalia, come and look! Another albatross seems to have joined us!" Turning to David, he said, "Sorry to interrupt, but I know Thalia's really interested in the wandering albatrosses."

Looking a little piqued but perhaps not wanting to argue with a passenger, David said, "Well, I can't compete with that! And besides, we are about to pick up the Auckland harbor pilot, and I have work to do. You might want to watch the pilot come aboard. Let's talk tomorrow, Thalia."

As Thalia and Nigel went to the rail to watch the activity surrounding the arrival of the pilot, a seaman arrived looking for David, who left hastily with him. When they were safely out of earshot, Nigel said, "I know it's late, and I know there's not another albatross, but would you sit down with me for a while? I would really like to talk to you about something."

"There's not another albatross? You were lying to us? Nigel, stop trying to protect me! I'm a big girl!" She turned away from him, looking over the rail and saying, "But I do appreciate your kindness, all you've done--introducing me to your group, including me at the table, making me feel befriended." Thoughtfully now, she said, "I suspect you know that David Springer propositioned me this evening. How did you guess?"

"Any man can see what he is, Thalia! I bet he targets one girl on every trip for his 'attentions'."

Grinning, he continued, "I saw him reach under the table, and guessed he was passing a note to you, or perhaps... umm... being familiar."

"Oh, ugh! Like those perverts on the train when it's crowded? Well, I guess in a way--he kept rubbing his leg against mine, and I didn't know what to do. Why do girls blame themselves when things like that happen? Did I encourage him?"

"Well, maybe a little, you know. You looked pretty smitten when he showed up."

"Oh, now I'm mortified! Is everyone laughing at me?"

"Only sometimes. Mostly they're thinking about themselves. Just keep on being yourself and everything'll be fine, Thalia."

By now, the pilot had boarded *Oriana* and his launch was pulling away. The illuminating floodlight was extinguished, and Thalia suddenly noticed the absence of the albatross. "I suppose they don't follow ships into harbor, do they?"

"I don't know," answered Nigel "but could we sit down and talk? I'm tired, but if I let this chance go, I might not get another chance to talk to you before Vancouver."

Thalia, curious now, agreed. "Alright, do you think the bar's still open? We could talk there, and I would love a drink."

As they moved toward the bar, where there were still late revelers, Thalia felt the engines slow as the ship entered the outer harbor and the swells of the open Pacific died away. Finding a table by the window, they watched the lighted buoys of the shipping lane flashing as *Oriana* passed and the first lights of the land began to show.

"Another country!" she said. "Do you know how much Australians want to see the world? We are so isolated that it's easy to be provincial and we all want to get out and see the things we've read about, and drink wine and sit in cafes and be worldly. So, what do you want to talk to me about? Apart from warning me about David Springer."

"I want you to know about me. The others treat me like their little brother, but I am going places, and I want you to come with me..."

"Nigel, this is so sudden!" Thalia said laughingly, mocking his seriousness. "Where are you going? I can't decide until I have more information."

"I'm a serious actor. I'm not going to be staying in these dated 'drawing room comedy' bits forever. These things are dead--the new playwrights are talking about real life, real problems people have, not more of the 'tennis-anyone, Dahling' silliness."

"I've heard of the new movement--*gritty reality, life's tough*. But people still like amusing light plays, don't they? They want to relax and be entertained at the theatre, not lectured. The new plays sound pretty hard work!"

"Life's hard work, Thalia! And this group--Amelia, Charmian, Julian--they're good actors, but they're limited by their material. And they're too old, too type-cast to make the change to serious theatre. They'll be alright, have work till they retire, but they're definitely a dying breed. And I'm not going to die with them, I'm going to make a mark. Shakespeare! Shaw! The new ones like John Osborne, Bertolt Brecht, T.S. Eliot, some of the old ones too, like Sheridan or Oscar Wilde. The poetry of the English language! Or foreign plays--Molière, Chekhov, perhaps American plays--Tennessee Williams in London! Do you know when I began to fall in love with you?"

"You are NOT in love with me, you are just bored and a bit caught up in the romance of travelling."

"No, you're wrong. It was when you began to spout poetry at me. No-one in my life has ever done that before. I was sitting there quietly in the middle of the night watching a bird, when suddenly an ancient Irish warrior queen, Aoife perhaps, barefoot, pyjama-clad, tangled red hair down her back, appeared and started to tell me about the death of hope and Coleridge's mystical poem, while this enormous bird soared back and forth above the limitless ocean and we seemed to be travelling in another world."

"I was not wearing pyjamas!" Stopping, she corrected herself, "I mean... I was fully dressed! And my hair wasn't tangled. Nigel, I'm going to bed. You're squiffy, and you'll wake up with a hangover, and not remember anything in the morning. Warrior queen, indeed! How silly!"

"No, you've got it wrong, Thalia! I *will* remember this, and so will you. I won't let you go."

"Well, mister Nigel, that's where you're wrong. I am not going to get involved with any actor-poet. Too many feckless Irishmen in my family already. I chose Douglas. Goodnight." And she jumped up from her chair and left the bar, heading for the stairs.

Nigel was faster than she; reaching the door first, he prevented her from opening it, and grabbed her hand saying, "This has never happened to me before. Please don't marry Douglas. Come with me to London."

Thalia, removing her hand from his grasp, uncertain now of how to handle this situation, said "Nigel, it's too late. I love Douglas and I made a promise that I plan to keep. I don't want to hurt you, but it's just not going to happen." Brushing back the dark red hair that had fallen in front of her face, she said crossly, "It's really late, and we'll be in port soon. I'm going to bed." She pushed past him, letting the door slam behind her.

And Nigel had to be content with that, for the moment

Chapter Nine

The Newcomer

The "drinkies" in Julian's cabin the night following the Auckland stop were lavish although the snacks were not, and Table 35's group was feeling no pain by the time it arrived in the dining salon. Julian's manner became more grave, more ponderous, as the whiskies took effect. As they arrived at the table, he was instructing Nigel how to kiss the hand of a lady... "As an aspiring romantic lead, you must know how to do this. You rest the lady's hand gently in your right hand, turning it to face down if it's not offered that way, then raise it slowly toward your lips, inclining your head and shoulders to meet it halfway. Then, you make the kiss from a fraction above the hand, gently miming the action of a kiss. NEVER touch the lips to the hand. Straightening, still holding the hand, you put your heels together--no, no, you do not click them. You are not Prussian! Bow, say "Madame," and release the hand. If she is American, she will say 'Oh, my!' and giggle, but most Europeans are not impressed by the action and will judge how well it's performed."

As the English girls arrived, he insisted that Nigel must kiss each girl's hand, giving him marks for the performance and asking the women for their comments. It took a few moments for the group to realize that there was a newcomer at the table. Still playing the part of the leader, the arbiter of the group, Julian began to apologize but was cut off by Amelia, who said "Oh, for heaven's sake, Julian, simmer down! We can introduce ourselves, but first let's ask the gentleman to tell us who he is," and, giving the newcomer a lascivious look (Julian's pink gins had been generously poured), waited for him to speak. As Amelia stood there, poised on her extremely high heels, the first rollers of the open Pacific hit the ship and tipped her onto the stranger's lap.

"Well, hello!" he said, "I don't believe we've been introduced. I'm John Ridd of Doone Valley Farm. May I know your name?"

Amelia, redfaced, embarrassed, and scrambling to stand up, looked to Julian and said "Julian, will you do the honors, please?"

Genially, Julian said, "with the greatest of pleasure, although I suppose we should wait until our host the purser joins us. This though seems like an emergency, and we must extricate Amelia from her embarrassing position. Mr. Ridd, may I present Miss Amelia Sims, lead actress of our small but distinguished troupe? I see that she has made an impression on you already."

Ridd, nut-brown complexion and merry brown eyes, chuckled and replied, "Such an enthusiastic welcome,

Miss Sims. Very pleased to meet you! Could I meet everyone else as soon as we all get settled?"

They sat down, and one by one introduced themselves; Nigel, the last, said, "I suppose our host, David Springer, will be here soon, but while we are waiting for him, Mr. Ridd, could you tell us something of yourself? Are you a New Zealander?"

The newcomer started to speak, but was interrupted by the arrival of David Springer, with Thalia following at a distance. "Oh, good," he said "I am pleased to see you all welcoming our new tablemate." Thalia, with his attention diverted from her by the new passenger, took the seat next to Nigel at the far side of the table from where she had been seated by the purser at the previous meal. Looking around the table, David said, "Thalia, you have moved yourself and now my seating plan is all muddled. Come back over here, and let Mr. Ridd have that seat." *One kiss, my bonny sweetheart, I'm after a prize to-night.*

Flushing but smiling, she remained seated and said "I think Dorrie should sit there, she loves horses, and Mr. Ridd told us a minute ago that he raises horses on his farm. Dorrie, would you like to sit there?" Dorrie, with a small smirk showing she knew what Thalia was up to, nodded and moved to the seat between Springer and Ridd, while the purser gave Thalia a brief glare before turning his attention to the whole table as the stewards arrived to take dinner orders.

Then, with his official welcoming manner firmly in place, David said, “We use first names here. John, I hope you don’t mind! Can you tell us something about yourself now, while we wait for dinner to arrive? Are you a New Zealander?”

Speaking with the same flat accent as most Australians and New Zealanders, Ridd said, “Oh, first names are fine--we’re a pretty casual lot, us Kiwis. Yeah, born and raised on South Island. Family originally from Devon, long time ago. Established Doone Valley Farm in the nineteenth century. Merino sheep mostly, they’re good wool producers, do well in a temperate climate. Dad got started breeding horses for harness racing for fun about forty years ago, then I got into it too. That’s about all there is to tell.”

“Harness racing?” asked Charmian, “Is that like horse and cart races? I’m sorry not to know.”

Before John Ridd could answer, Dorrie said,“Charmian, have you ever been to the trots? That’s harness racing, and today I was told all about it while we were in Auckland.”

Ridd spoke up, "This young lady is right. New Zealand loves the trots! They race with the jockey in a light two-wheeled cart called a sulky. And some of our horses are going to the States now, winning racing prizes like mad. That's what I'm doing--taking a couple of our horses to sell over there."

"I'm Dorrie Magnus, John, and my family is known as ''the horsey Magnuses'. I hope we can talk some more about your horses and Doone Valley Farm. Are they on board? Can I see them?"

Watching this, Thalia remembered Dorrie's remarks about The Fleet's disappointment with Australian men; perhaps John Ridd was a prospect for one of the young fishers. The food arrived and David ordered wine for the table, saying, "I can't stay for the whole meal. Lots to do getting all the new passengers organized, so I'll say goodnight in a few minutes and see you all tomorrow. Thalia, I need to talk to you about your cabin. We have to move you to another deck, so please stop by my office after dinner."

As the purser left the table, conversation became general, with the girls telling of their explorations of Auckland. Thalia was quiet, wondering what was going on with her cabin and David's request that she go to his office. Charmian offered to go with her, and she gratefully accepted. *Yet if they press me sharply and harry me through the day. Then look for me by moonlight, Watch for me by moonlight, I'll come to thee by moonlight*

The English girls left next, taking John Ridd with them in a gust of laughter and teasing, and heading to the ballroom. Thalia and Charmian walked together to the purser's office. When they arrived, David met them at the reception desk and took them to Thalia's new quarters; a steward would be sent to move her things, he said, and she could sleep there tonight. The new cabin was one deck down, with a porthole through which she could see the ocean, and a small bathroom with a shower. No sharing the communal washroom for me, thought Thalia. But how could she afford it, she asked. David replied that he knew that her fiancé had wanted to book a better cabin for her, but there had been nothing available. Now, something had opened up – TaDa! It was hers! He handed her the key and left.

"This is wonderful!" gushed Thalia, "I don't have to go to the washroom down the hall and carry all my stuff. Douglas didn't tell me he tried to get a single cabin for me. Isn't it lucky that David knew about it?"

Charmian rolled her eyes. "Thalia, don't be so naïve. P&O's a huge shipping company! I doubt very much that David knew about it. Be careful!" *Though hell should bar the way!*

“I’m not a baby, Charmian! You all think I’m innocent, and I’m not. I am thoroughly grown-up, and completely modern, and I can handle David Springer.” She laughed and sat on the bed and bounced for a moment. “But he is kind of... umm... attractive, isn’t he? Do you really think he’s married? That would be a pity. Amelia said I need experience, and I think I might use him for practice. What do you think?"

"Don't play with fire, Thalia. You might get burned.” *King George’s men came marching, marching, marching, Up to the old inn door.*

Chapter Ten
Shipboard Romance

Thalia spent the night in her new digs, enjoying the space and the bathroom. The view of the ocean through the porthole was limited, but at least one could see out so it didn't feel as claustrophobic as an inside cabin. *Oriana* would reach Fiji the day after tomorrow, and after a brief stop, would head toward the international date line and the equator. The weather was fine, and the ship's northerly course took them past several small nameless atolls, each a minute treeless island with a lagoon formed by a ring of coral and barely above water at high tide. I wonder whether the albatross will stay with us when we cross the equator, Thalia thought, or will a bird from the northern hemisphere take its place? I don't think there are wandering albatrosses in the northern hemisphere. Will this bird look for another ship to follow on its return journey south?

The morning was uneventful. The purser didn't show up at the table for breakfast. Thalia spent the morning in the library where she wrote a letter to Douglas to be mailed in Suva. "*Darling*," she wrote, "*I have a new wonderful cabin! Thank you so much for requesting a better one when you were booking passage for me! One suddenly became available, and the purser moved me to it when we left Auckland. It's much larger than the first one and has its own bathroom – such luxury! It is almost large enough that we could share it, if you were here. But it won't be long until we are really sharing our lives, and I can't wait! I feel as if I have waited all my life for you, and the thought of making our lives together--really together—is wonderful!"*

"Ah, there you are, Thalia. You are the most difficult person to find sometimes! Why are you hiding in this dusty old room?" Amelia asked, settling herself down in the chair to the library, next to Thalia and lighting a cigarette. "Alright, alright, I won't light it!" she said to the library steward as he looked disapprovingly at her cigarette "Oh, I see, you're writing to your hero! Well, you can't post a letter for two more days, so come out and play. This Mr. Ridd is a charmer, and I think he has an eye for little Dorrie! Come and see! The flirting is heavy, and my guess is they'll be in bed together before morning. He's got a single cabin, David says."

"Amelia! You are outrageous! Dorrie's a nice girl from a good family!"

"Ho! They're the worst! They've been repressed for so long you can't hold 'em back when they get off the leash! And when are you going to do something about David Springer's urge for you, missy? He'd be good practice for you, you know."

Since this was exactly what Thalia had said to Charmian, it was difficult to contradict, but she tried. "How do you know he has an urge for me, Amelia? Can you read minds? And I'm engaged to be married, and not interested in playing around."

"Oh, really? The temperature in the dining room the other night was so high between you two that I thought the fire sprinklers might come on! Lose that useless virginity! But – just to be sure, are you prepared? Don't want any complications, if you know what I mean."

"I'm not going to discuss this with you any more, Amelia. It's not your business, but if you must know, yes, I'm prepared for marriage. I'm not completely ignorant." With that, Thalia stood up and stalked out as impressively as her five foot two inches allowed. I am prepared, she thought, I started on this new pill before I left Australia, so Douglas and I can have time together and can decide for ourselves when to begin a family. Modernity! Just as well Mum didn't know though. She wouldn't approve. Makes things too easy, I guess.

She found Table 35's group already assembled in the stern bar, and Amelia sauntered up just as Thalia sat down at the edge of the laughing group. Amelia took the chair next to her, seating herself in a flurry of belongings--a little bag containing cigarettes and long jade holder, sun lotion, large straw hat, hot pink to match her shoulder-baring sundress, and a book. Crossing her long legs, she pulled her full skirt above her knees to display their shapeliness, ankles accentuated by the stiletto-heeled sandals she wore despite yesterday's unfortunate accident. The bar steward noticed her arrival, as did almost every man on the deck and, casting an appreciative glance at her legs, delivered her gin and tonic and waited for the small ceremony of lighting her cigarette.

"Well, well, well," said Julian, "here is our Amelia, the focus of our admiration, the starry genius of our little company. And what is this object that she carries? Could it be a book? Does she--can she--read?"

Amelia shrugged. "Julian, don't be such a bore. You know perfectly well that I can and do read. How do you think I learn all my lines?"

"I'm not at all certain that you do learn them, dearie. In the first act one night last season, you picked up my cue and gave about half my part before you slowed down enough for me to stop you. Since it was my speech complaining about your unfaithfulness to me, it confused the audience quite a lot!"

Julian and Amelia continued to bicker lazily, with Nigel joining in from time to time. Thalia watched Dorrie and John, and realized that Amelia had been right about them. Dorrie, her brown hair no longer pulled back into a ponytail but curling softly about her young face, was very engaged in the conversation, and much prettier than Thalia had realized; John Ridd appeared enthralled by her. His eyes caressed her, never left her face, and he seemed not to hear any of the conversations around them. A shipboard romance, she wondered, or something more serious.

The steward with the little xylophone gong passed by – ten minutes to lunch, the gong announced. Amelia left the bar with Julian, and Nigel moved to sit next to Thalia. "Are you alright?" he asked. "Was Amelia bothering you? I saw her going into the library while you were writing a letter. I knew you were there but I didn't think you wanted to be social."

Thalia thought to herself that this is a considerate man, kind and thoughtful. "Oh, I was writing to Douglas, telling him about the new cabin. But I'd pretty much finished when she arrived." Then, looking toward Dorrie and John, she smiled at Nigel, and said, "Remember we talked about shipboard romances the night we met on the deck and saw the albatross the first time? How sweet and intense they can be, but how sometimes they wither really fast on land?" He laughed and nodded, and Thalia continued, "This one looks really intense, doesn't it? Any guesses as to its endurance?"

“Looks like the real thing, to me. Like my feeling for you. Don’t forget that, Thalia”.

“Friends only, don't forget I'm engaged! I’m engaged, but I do want you to be my friend.”

Smilingly he agreed, and arm in arm, they went to the dining room. The purser didn’t appear at lunch. Neither did Dorrie and John.

Table 35’s group reassembled in the ballroom after lunch. “Pretty girls needed to help the horses get to the finish line at the races tonight, and this P&O tub is filled with the prettiest! Help us put them to work!” Amelia’s steward, wearing an open-necked white shirt with sleeves rolled up, porkpie hat on the back of his head and a large cigar in his mouth, stood on a box with a capacious bookmaker’s bag on his shoulder and straw strewn on the deck around him. “Get your votes here, fill in the name of your favorite lovely, and place it in this feed barrel. Only one vote per person, you’ve got fifteen minutes till we draw the names, and no buying extra votes! One man, one vote only”

At the far end of the room stood six small wooden horses with fabric manes and tails, a crouching cutout of a jockey in bright silks on each slender back. Attached to the nose of each was a hook with a line extending the length of the dance floor to a large fishing rod and reel in front of a ballroom chair. “Ladies and gentlemen! Six neddies, six reels, and six chairs – who will fill these chairs and help the jockeys win the first race tonight? “Come on, mates, choose the prettiest fillies for this job!” There was neighing from the horses, some prancing, helped by the group of stewards standing by. “Let’s get this done so we can get on with the action-- these nags are getting impatient.”

The ballroom was stiflingly hot and noisy, and Thalia felt she needed air, so she signaled to Julian that she would be back soon and left the ballroom. Up on the stern deck, the salty air was refreshing and the albatross in its perfect metronomic rhythm continued swooping across the ship’s wake. As she stood at the rail feeling the ship’s rise and fall, David Springer appeared. “Thalia, I hoped I would find you here! I was afraid though that you would be at the race–preparation below. It’s a big night, Race Night! We only do it once on the whole voyage.”

Thalia turned to him, saying “I was afraid *you* wouldn’t be here. I really want to thank you for my new cabin. Can you come for a drink there wlth me after the races get under way tonight?"

Chapter Eleven

Lessons with David

Thalia nervously tidied the cabin as she waited for David. The bed had been folded down by the steward, ready for her to slip under the covers. Should I remake it, she wondered. Does it seem suggestive this way? What can I give him to drink? I don't have anything but water, and the only glass is my toothbrush mug. Oh, this is a disaster! Why did I get myself into this? What was I thinking? This dress is too modest. Should I change to something more revealing? Well, I don't have anything like that anyway, so...

She was saved from her doubts by a soft knock at the door. She called out "Come in", and David Springer entered, smiling confidently and carrying a slender bag. The bag clinked softly, and he pulled out two glasses and a bottle, saying "Thalia! I am so glad you asked me to come. Do you like champagne? Sorry there are no orchids like you would get with your bubbly at the Moana Hotel in Hawaii!"

Sitting on the chair near the bed, he pulled out a pack of cigarettes and offered her one. *CravenA*, she noticed, the servicemen's cheap brand and not an upper class brand like *Gitanes* or *Sobranie,* and not even the respectable middle class *Rothmans* — odd choice. She shook her head and remained standing, feeling less and less confident in her plan. Sensing her unease, he said, "What can I do for you? You seem so nervous--I won't hurt you, I just want to be close to you. I hoped you would answer my note the other night but you never did. Can we start again?"

"David," she began "you know I am getting married in Vancouver? I'm engaged, and I plan to be faithful to my fiancé."

"You aren't married yet, and I feel sure you felt that lightning bolt when we met. Surely there would be no harm in a little pleasure before you make that serious commitment?"

Oh dear, thought Thalia, I am losing control of the situation. Must keep going now though. "Well, that's sort of what I wanted to talk to you about." She gulped and stopped, then continued, "I would like you to teach me... umm... what to do... how to be pleasing... all those things. Would you be interested in helping me?"

"You are asking me to prepare you for... your husband's... er... attentions?" David asked.

Nodding, she said uncertainly, "Amelia said I need experience, and I think she's right. But I don't know how to get any. Douglas and I haven't... umm... well, I was living at home, you know, and there wasn't much privacy and... I feel very naive, and it's really hard to talk about this."

Gently, he said "Thalia, are you asking me to teach you to make love? Or to have sex? There's a difference, you know. I can teach you about sex, about having fun, show you some things that will give pleasure, bolster your confidence, but the love part you and Douglas will have to build together. Do you understand?"

He's kind, she thought. I didn't expect that. "I suppose so. Are you married?"

"Yes. And my wife does not misunderstand me. In fact, she understands me very well. I am not looking to persuade anyone to go to bed with me if they don't want to, I intend to stay married but... well, it's a big ocean, a lot of nights alone, and a host of willing attractive women... and I would be charmed to help you. Shall we start now?"

"I'm a virgin. Does that matter? Do men know if a girl's a virgin when they... ?"

He chuckled. "To most modern men it doesn't matter unless they're members of a royal house fulfilling dynastic obligations. Does that apply to Douglas?"

It was Thalia's turn to laugh. "No. He's thoroughly modern, a man of the times, and proud of it. But this all seems very clinical, no romance to it at all. I hoped there would be some moonlight, some roses, some illusions."

"I'll take you to the Moana Hotel for dinner when we get to Hawaii. Dinner under the banyan tree on Waikiki Beach, pink tablecloths, little gold chairs, orchids in the champagne glasses, Don Ho singing "*Tiny Bubbles... tiny bubbles in the wine*". The food's not great but the romance is thick. Virginity doesn't stand a chance! One last question before we begin. Are you prepared?"

"Prepared? Oh, you mean prepared. Yes, I take a little pill every day so there won't be any consequences. It's the very latest thing!"

"Okay," David said. "No consequences, physical or emotional. Do we both understand that this is a friendly agreement which stops at the shore?"

"Yes" said Thalia, laughing, relieved. She had done it, achieved her purpose. "But please don't tell anyone! And stop flirting with me in public! Amelia's already suspicious."

Then she thought--how can I do this? How can I be so light about something as important as this--giving my virginity to this stranger. But no-one's going to know except me and David, and I don't think he would tell because he has a lot to lose too.

He walked over to the bed and sat down. "Come over here and we can sit together. We'll just sit, and we'll go as slowly as you like; I will stop when you tell me to, just trust me."

She did as he suggested; putting his arm around her shoulders, he pulled her close to him. She leaned in, turning her face to him to receive his kiss. His hands went to her hair, to pull out the pins which held it piled on her head. "Laugh, Thalia, enjoy being young and desirable! Let that lovely red hair down, I am at your service, Mademoiselle."

Chapter Twelve

Graduation

Thalia's virginity was gone by Fiji, her innocence by Honolulu.

Sated, she lay in bed in her cabin the morning after the ship left Hawaii, watching David Springer dress in his British merchant marine officer's tropical garb of white Bermuda shorts, white shirt with navy blue tie, and knee-length white socks. "Come back to bed, David" she said sleepily, "It's too early to get up. Let's talk about dinner at the Moana and the delightful dessert course, mmmmmm, so romantic--let's turn the ship round and do it again."

Leaning over the bed, he kissed her and said, "No, I'd love to but lots to do today. New passengers came aboard yesterday, everybody needs something from the purser's office. Glad my steward remembered to bring my fresh uniform and put it in your closet while we were ashore."

"What?" She sat up, holding the tangled sheet to try to cover herself, one small breast showing at the side, and began to cry. "Your steward was HERE? He knew to bring your stuff to MY cabin? Then he must know about us! Are people talking about us? Oh, how awful!"

“Don’t be such a goose! Of course people know, but mainly the officers and stewards. Unless the passengers are very friendly with one of the crew, they aren’t likely to know.”

“Amelia has a bar steward who visits her room, I know. She’s always pretty well-informed about things going on in the cabins. I bet she knows, and she’ll tell everyone. We have to stop!”

"A bit late to think of that now, don’t you think? And just what do you think she’s doing with the bar steward in her cabin--playing Scrabble? Most people are jealous! And why stop--might as well continue, since the cat’s out of the bag anyway. Unless you aren’t having a good time. You seemed to be enjoying it quite a lot, I thought.”

“I feel so cheap. How can I face Douglas?”

“Don’t tell him. That’s what you planned, wasn’t it? So… what has changed?

“Now people will know, and they will think I’m not a nice girl!”

“Oh, grow up! You asked for experience. You got experience. But you weren’t entirely honest with me, were you? You didn’t admit that you felt that thunderbolt too the day we met, and that the “experience” was really an excuse. You wanted me in your bed just as much as I wanted to be there."

"I hate you! Go away."

"Only four more nights till Vancouver." he said as he approached the door. "See you here after the dance tonight." The pillow hit the door as it closed behind him.

She lay in bed for a while, reflecting on the situation. At last, she admitted to herself that he was right. She had been deceptive and had used the excuse of her quest for experience in order to begin an affair with the purser. I suppose I should end it, she thought, but there are only four days left on the voyage. I don't want to stop yet. I just hope word doesn't get to Douglas, although it doesn't seem very likely that it would. And I would deny everything, if it did.

Heigh Ho, she thought, I have come a long way from little Thalia, cherished, innocent, Catholic daughter. Time to get up and face the dining salon. At least Amelia doesn't usually show up for breakfast.

The dining room was crowded. People were chattering about their adventures in Hawaii the previous day and making plans for the remainder of the voyage. John Ridd and Dorrie made an appearance, holding hands and sitting close together, tremulous with love and honey-toasted with sex. Looks like Dorrie achieved her aim, found her horse-loving Antipodean, and is bringing him home to the family. Good on her! Will Douglas and I look like that in our first days together, wondered Thalia, doubting it.

Amelia arrived at the table. "Good morning, everyone." she drawled as she waited for the steward to pull her chair out for her. "How was Hawaii for you all? And did everyone sleep well last night?" There was a general chorus of positive response, then she directed her attention to Thalia. "Thalia? How about you? Are you sleeping well in your little private quarters? Enjoying it, are you?"

Nigel looked up from his toast and marmalade, saying, "Amelia, how lovely to see you looking so winsome so early! You don't usually honor us with your presence at breakfast. Why don't you park your broomstick, sit down and get on with your gruel or whatever potion sustains you for the day ahead, and let us do the same for ourselves."

Isabelle giggled, but her sister gave her a stern look and she subsided. Dorrie and John were aware only of one another, but Julian looked sympathetically at Thalia and said "Of course she's enjoying her private cabin! Don't you like yours, Amelia? The freedom to do what you like, when you like?"

Thalia realized that they knew, all of them. They know I am sleeping with David Springer, and they have probably been discussing it. While she wondered what to do, how to handle this, Charmian spoke.

To Thalia, Charmian was sometimes kind, but mostly seemed remote, brittle with her shrewd watchful eyes; it was surprising to hear her say, "Thalia, I am not sure you know how much we all admire you. It is so courageous of you to leave your home and travel so far alone to marry the man you love, and we want to have a little farewell for you on the last night. Would that be alright with you?"

Before Thalia could answer, Julian joined in. "We've been talking about it for a couple of days now. Just the group at this table, plus anyone else you would want to include. Any special stewards perhaps?" His eyes twinkled a little as he said this, and everyone at the table laughed. Except for Thalia.

No-one looked at Amelia, who was drumming her long red fingernails on the table, a petulant expression on her face. Finally, she spoke. "Yes, our little Thalia has certainly grown up a lot on this voyage! You've acquired some... um... sophistication, I think, and some knowledge of the world outside provincial Australia. Congrats, my dear! Quite an achievement. I wonder if the legendary Douglas would be pleased."

Amelia is challenging me, thought Thalia. She wants me to be defensive, weak and apologetic, so that she can feel victorious in this weird contest she has with me in her mind. Ignoring Amelia, she answered Julian's question, "Oh, how lovely! I would love that, and I know Douglas would be happy too. I am sorry he won't be able to meet the people who have made this trip so wonderful for me but I will certainly tell him all about it." Well, maybe not quite all, she thought.

Chapter Thirteen
End of the Voyage

The ship's newspaper, slipped under the door in the early morning, had announced "*Last Night on the Pacific Tonight! Wear your fanciest clothes and join us in the Aft Deck Bar at 6 for a Celebration!*"

Thalia pulled out the single evening dress she had in her luggage and its matching shoes and evening bag. As she dressed for the evening, she wondered what her friends had planned for her farewell celebration. Honestly, she thought, I would rather not have to be smiling and gay. I am looking forward to seeing Douglas, to starting our lives together, but I have some doubts. Not doubts about Douglas, not really, just hesitation. I suppose they are the same thing, but I don't doubt Douglas, I just want to be sure he's right for me. I think Amelia was right about experience, although not exactly in the way she intended. But I have finished with David. I ended it last night, told him not to come tonight, said that I am respecting our agreement--the whole thing stops with the shore, and I will go on with my life as if nothing had ever happened. He agreed that it is over, The End.

But, she thought, is it possible to go on as if nothing had happened? When a stone is thrown into the water, do the rings expand forever? I can't un-throw the stone. What happens to the energy of that throwing? Am I changed forever by this action, this affair, this "experience"? David is gone, but I threw a stone and changed myself. And Douglas--will I change him also? Can I really pretend the affair with David never took place?

Sobered by her thoughts and questions, she finished dressing; there was a light tap on the door, and she opened it to Nigel, dinner-jacketed, black-tied, and leading-man handsome. I have been discounting Nigel, she thought, putting him down as too young, too inexperienced, to be a serious romantic interest. For me, or anyone else, but he is notably attractive in his own way. Oh, well, too late now.

Nigel offered his arm, told her she looked lovely, and, appearing to accept his role as Thalia's squire for the evening and nothing more, escorted her to the party in the Aft Deck Bar.

"You're very quiet this evening, Miss Thalia" remarked Julian. "Everything alright with you? Can I help at all?"

Thalia declined, feeling that an offer of help from Julian was somewhat equivalent to such an offer from Caesar Augustus, although better than an offer from Amelia, Livia to his Caesar. But then taking courage from his seeming kindness, said, "Well, perhaps. I have doubts.

Doubts about my future, about Douglas, and about my maturity. Perhaps my mother was right!"

"Aaah, I see. The growing process, the detachment from mother, the maturing realization that the world is much more complicated than you had thought. Welcome to adulthood, Thalia."

She looked at him, trying to assess his meaning. "Is that what it is, really? Have I been growing up on this trip, leaving my country, my family, and my young self behind? It doesn't feel like that. It feels like everything has shifted focus, and left only shards of memories behind that mean nothing. Tomorrow I will see Douglas again, first time in a year. I'm not the same person I was a year ago. Has he changed too?"

"You can't answer that now. Only time will tell you that. So, why not relax and enjoy tonight--the music, the romance of an ocean voyage, the making of new memories. Let's dance. May I have this dance, madame?" Laughing, she assented and they moved onto the dance floor to mingle with the other dancers as the band played sentimental old songs and the ship left the open waters of the Pacific Ocean to begin the long intricate passage into Vancouver Harbor.

Nothing marred the evening for Thalia; Amelia smoldered quietly in the corner, smoking Sobranies, the gold-tipped black cigarettes fashionable among the sophisticates of the era and constantly calling her steward for more drinks and snacks for the table, but saying nothing in particular. "The cigarettes are black like her heart! But I think she's been defanged," whispered Nigel to Thalia as they danced, "She seems a bit unhappy, doesn't she?"

Dorrie and John surfaced again, announcing that they planned to marry as soon as they could on arrival in England. "What a surprise!" exclaimed Isabelle to her sister Sibyl, "But just as well he's making an honest woman of her. Her family would disown her otherwise. No fallen women in the horsey Magnus clan!"

Addresses were exchanged, promises made to meet in London when Thalia made it there, invitations extended to visit Thalia and Douglas when they got settled in Washington, and a wedding gift from the ship's store was presented--a handsome clock, capable of showing the time in three different places in the world. "So you'll always know the time in London, Melbourne, and Washington!" said Charmian, "once you work out how to set it correctly. We couldn't figure it out."

Last farewells made, the party broke up around midnight. Nigel and Thalia remained on deck to watch as the ship slowed its engines and its forward motion to allow the Vancouver Harbor pilot to come aboard to guide the ship safely through the complex shoals and twists of the harbor entrance.

As they stood at the rail together, Nigel said, "Thalia, I won't ask you again to run away with me to London. Not because I don't want that, but because I understand now that you won't do it. But don't forget what I said."

"Nigel, it's been a lot of fun, this trip together! I have loved getting to know you and the troupe. Well, all but Amelia! I won't forget you, and when I come to London, maybe we can have lunch together and remember the albatross and the conga line and Julian's drinkies, and you can practice kissing my hand."

"Don't forget to let me know. I have an offer of a new play in London. Auditions as soon as I get there, and it's a real play in a real theatre. In London! When you come, we'll go to The Ivy for dinner after the performance, and strut a little. I'm on my way, and I wish I could take you with me, but... So, goodbye for now, Aoife, red-haired Irish warrior queen."

The ship began to move forward again under command of the pilot, and the lights of Lion's Gate Bridge appeared. They passed under the high bridge to enter the inner harbor, and Thalia's voyage into adulthood was almost over. She gripped the polished wooden rail of *Oriana's* deck as if holding onto the past, but in her mind eager to meet the future. Noticing her hands, she realized that her nails were short, unpolished, a little bitten and cuticles broken, not like the hands of Amelia and Charmian, smooth with manicured lacquered nails, the hands of adult women. She wore her grandmother's ring on her right hand; the soft old silver ring with the Celtic cross was dented and marred, worn before her by two generations of women; it was the ring of a daughter, she thought, and her hands the hands of a child. Douglas would soon place another ring on her left hand, and she would no longer be only a daughter. So, now the end of the voyage, and only the reunion with Douglas remained, and a manicure.

Chapter Fourteen

Marriage

When the ship docked in Vancouver, Douglas waited on the quay, ardent and imperious. Thalia could catch a glimpse of him from time to time through a window as she moved from official desk to official desk working her way through Customs and Immigration, while he fumed and paced on the quay. She saw David Springer descend the gangway and stop to talk with him. They chatted for a few minutes, then shook hands and parted. David went down the quay and out of sight, while Douglas stood quietly for a moment or two before resuming his pacing. At last, the formalities were done and visitors were permitted to board. As he started up the gangway, she hurried out on deck and waited there where he would arrive, ready for their first meeting in more than a year.

He looks different, she thought, as he got closer. He seems a bit older, his chin stronger, more determined, and there's even a hint of jowls on his cheeks. He doesn't look like the man I agreed to marry. He ran up, his long legs carrying him in powerful strides across to her, gave her a quick peck on the cheek, and said "Well, Thalia! Good to see you. Where's your stuff? Hope you don't have too much. Let's go."

Not even a hug, she thought, but said nothing. Quickly she identified her luggage – the suitcase with her clothing and intimate things, plus the trunk with the large "Not Wanted on Voyage" label that had emerged from the ship's hold for Customs inspection. It contained her trousseau, the small number of things she had brought from home, the wedding gifts, the lovingly-chosen linens and pretty household items intended to furnish their first home together.

She longed to ask what he and David had said to one another, but didn't dare to give anything away by asking. If it were something bad, I will certainly hear, and if it's not, then I will never hear anything. I hope I will never know, she thought.

"Over here, hurry up." Douglas shouted rudely to a porter and directed him to his car, which stood in the parking area, then taking Thalia's arm, led her to the car. "No time to waste today, Thalia. Gotta be at the registry office by 11 o'clock for the wedding, then back to the US Consulate for your immigration visa. Time for sentiment after that. Let's go." Too overwhelmed to protest, Thalia was swept along, but not without regrets for the lacy white dress she had in her luggage for her wedding day and for the lack of flowers and music. And romance.

So, Thalia and Douglas married in Vancouver, Canada on July 12, 1965, spending their honeymoon traveling across the United States in Douglas's small auto. They stopped in Wisconsin so that Thalia and his family could meet, then continued to Washington where they planned to live while Douglas worked for The Capital Beacon, a large politically liberal American newspaper.

The family and Thalia approved of each other, his parents being pleased that he had at last decided to settle down to adult life, his brother Peter pleased because he found Thalia's Australian independence and candor refreshing and amusing, and Thalia pleased that she had been so readily accepted.

"Doug," Peter said to his brother when they had a minute alone, "Good choice! She's delightful, but not at all what I expected."

"What did you expect, Peter? I'd like to know. It might give me a clue to what you think of me."

"Oh, I don't know. I guess I never really thought about it, but I suppose I expected an American, someone raised and educated here, and Thalia is a pleasant surprise. I keep thinking though of George Bernard Shaw's comment about English: '*England and America are two countries divided by a common language*', and I guess Australia as a Commonwealth member fits under that too. It's a big adjustment for someone young without much experience in another country."

"Oh, Shaw, that socialist prig. She'll be fine. Australians are tough and adaptable. Give her a couple of months and she'll settle down to learning to cook pancakes and burgers, and having babies. Once in a while though, GBS was right, like when he said '*Marriage is popular because it combines the maximum of temptation with the maximum of opportunity.*' Surprised I've heard of Shaw?"

In truth, Peter was surprised, since he thought his brother rather bourgeois and unread, with much of the family's inherent American conservatism. But he truly wished the couple well, hoping that Thalia would be able to bring Douglas to a more open and cosmopolitan view. He realized though that this would be a big task for a young woman just beginning to understand the culture of a new country vastly different from her own despite their shared language.

Thalia, for her part, was confused. Even the "liberals" in the United States seemed, to her Australian eyes, conservative and their refusal to consider that another country might offer a better way of doing things strange and prejudiced. Douglas shared this American view, she discovered. But other-wise the marriage was good, so far. Despite the impression made in their first hurried meeting on the ship, he was considerate of her needs, her preferences in the choice of a place to live and how to furnish it, and spent long hours with her seeking an apartment in their chosen location. The sex, she thought privately, could be more exciting. In the way of unfulfilled wives in her era, she felt that this reflected on some lack in herself and did not confide her feelings to Douglas, but thought of Amelia and simply wished that she had had more experience, and bought a little book which promised to help her to discreetly make things more interesting.

Altogether her life was pleasant, although Douglas's colleagues at the newspaper were mostly older than they and there wasn't much social contact there, but it was easy to make friends among the young residents of their apartment complex, and their social life blossomed. Douglas was working hard, keeping long hours at the office, and when Thalia began to be bored she joined the local amateur theatrical group. Mostly composed of members of the British and Commonwealth diplomatic colony, it was fun for her to meet compatriots and join in the efforts to present well-acted, interesting theatre. Washington in those days had only two professional theatres, and interest in the amateur productions was intense. They performed to sold-out audiences.

Thalia was amused by the thought that she was now in the same line of work as Julian, Charmian, Amelia, and Nigel, and she wrote to Julian to tell him. Notes came back from all but Amelia, telling her their London news and making delighted comments about her involvement in theatre. Douglas however didn't approve. "Thalia, actors aren't people like us. They're loose, rather like gypsies. They're not respectable members of society." Their morals were questionable, he continued. "I don't want them in the house—you never know what they might do!" and he did not want her involved with such people.

When Thalia responded that most of the people in the theatre group were members of the diplomatic community and could hardly be considered Bohemian, and that no-one so far had suggested that she might want to participate in an open marriage or tried to sell stolen goods to her, he relented and allowed her to continue, with the proviso that he would personally pick her up and bring her home at the conclusion of the evening.

Despite his misgivings though, Douglas came to some of the cast parties, and seemed to enjoy himself and fit in well with the group. A new actress joined the theatre company--Beryl, a young Englishwoman, pretty, blonde, with a curvaceous figure and a cheeky, seductive manner. Douglas's work responsibilities appeared to increase at this time, and there were numerous occasions when he couldn't take Thalia home, and she was free to leave under her own steam. He usually appeared an hour or so after she arrived home, in an excellent mood and eager to go to bed with her. His lovemaking was enthusiastic and more playful than previously, and pretty soon Thalia found herself pregnant. Apparently there had been a failure in the magical pills.

After much discussion, they decided that their apartment would be too small for them and the baby, and Thalia, with a real estate agent, searched for a small house in a close-in suburb. She hoped to find a freestanding house with a garden where a child could play, and dreamed of a tree for a swing and a lawn for croquet, envisioning herself stretched out in a *chaise longue*, wearing a fluttery white dress of fine cotton, and smelling of Elizabeth Arden's "Blue Grass" perfume, the popular scent of the day. She would have an interesting book and their charming children--by now her dream babies had multiplied--would play amicably beside her while she read.

A house was found, not freestanding but one of a short terrace of houses in the old colonial port city of Alexandria, newly fashionable with young families, who planned to renovate the old houses. The price was a little high for their budget, but Douglas's parents helped them to meet it, they acquired it and moved in. Although there was only a small garden in the back of the house, Thalia found it pleasant and full of possibility, and her head was full of plans for scented lilies, blossoming trees, and lush green lawns frequented by singing birds and pretty children, although the reality of her pregnancy combined with the drenching humidity of a Washington summer caused her to put most of these plans on hold.

Their first child, Daniel Douglas, was born in 1968. It was an easy birth for Thalia, and baby Daniel thrived from the beginning. He was a placid, cheerful baby, but the realities of child care and household responsibilities made it impossible for her to continue with the theatrical group. Douglas though seemed comfortable with the group now and had volunteered to work on several behind-the-scenes projects; Thalia was pleased that he had an interest outside his work. He continued to come home late in the evening, and his lovemaking with her was less enthusiastic, something she thought must be because she hadn't lost the baby weight, and she felt tired, overweight, and unattractive.

She dutifully maintained the family ties, both with her own family in Australia and with Douglas's family in Wisconsin. Douglas's parents and his brother Peter came for Daniel's first Christmas, Peter bringing with him a copy of the manuscript of his just-completed novel.

Peter, a shy and reserved man, asked her tentatively if she would care to read his novel, and knowing that she was a discerning reader, was interested in hearing her comments on his work. He gave no indication of whether or not he had approached a publisher with the book, but left a carbon copy of the manuscript with her, asking that she return it with her comments when she had finished. She found the work intensely moving, and was impressed by Peter's facility with both language and history.

Titled A Family's Pain, the fictional story was complex, telling of an old, settled American family, in the country since the earliest days of British settlement. Each generation had proudly sent men to fight for the country in its wars, from the War of Independence to the Korean War. They had lost sons and knew the bitterness of the loss of the promise of their young men, but had accepted these as the price of patriotism. Until now, until Vietnam. Their young men refused to go. Several of them left the US for Canada, others participated in angry demonstrations and draft-dodging maneuvers, none of them were prepared to support their country in what they considered an unjust and unnecessary war. Like many families, the parents were conflicted, alternately ashamed of this refusal but also proud of the determination shown by their children to fight for their beliefs. The war was ongoing, there was no resolution, and the book ended on a note of sadness and resignation.

"Peter, I am awestruck by your book," wrote Thalia. "It has touched my heart, and made me reflect on so much of what I am presently learning about American families, their history and pride." He never received her letter.

Before it arrived in Madison, he was killed in an auto accident. She gave the manuscript to Douglas to read; when he returned it, she kept it carefully among her most treasured belongings

Their family life in Washington went on, becoming a little dull and humdrum. Douglas seemed more and more preoccupied with his work, and began to travel on overseas assignments, leaving Thalia and Daniel alone in Alexandria for several months at a time. She started to wonder if there were someone else in his life, and when he returned from an assignment in London, she asked him as directly as she dared if he had been unfaithful.

“Douglas, is everything alright with you?” asked Thalia as they sat in the candlelit garden late one summer evening, leaf shadows moving around them in the warm breeze, the shifting light blurring facial expressions.

“What kind of question is that, Thalia?” he replied. “Why should something be wrong? Got something on your conscience?”

Sighing, Thalia thought--of course, Douglas's familiar belief that the best defense is a good offense. “No, not on mine, but I am wondering about you. I hear Beryl is back in London. I know you enjoyed her company, and thought you might have seen her there.”

“Thalia, why are you like this? Have I ever given you any reason to distrust me?
Again, Douglas on the defensive, she thought--answer a question with a question.

Of course you have, she thought, all those late nights, but carefully she said, “Oh, not really, but I just sense that something has changed.”

“Nothing’s changed. I’m just tired, overworked, I need a break. Why can’t you understand that?

Though suspecting that he was concealing something, Thalia knew that she too was hiding something and that for her to push too hard might be to raise Douglas’s suspicions and risk revealing the story of David Springer, so the topic was dropped.

Thalia arranged to send Daniel to a friend, and they took a long weekend in the tidewater of Virginia, where the play of light and shadow on the watery landscape pleased her sense of the dramatic. By now, she had lost the baby weight from her pregnancy with Daniel, and was slimmer and more beautiful in her early maturity than in her youth. Her dark red hair was long, and against the intense color of her hair, the creamy pallor of her skin and the transparent aquamarine of her eyes were striking. She wore her hair pinned up loosely, and had learned the seductive habit of beautiful women of every period of letting it down to flow over bare shoulders as she sat at her mirror in the bedroom. She planned carefully for this weekend and their lovemaking seemed to regain some of its earlier intensity; she returned to Alexandria reassured of the stability of her marriage.

Chapter Fifteen

Moving, 1971

"So, Thalia, how would you like to live in Europe?" asked Douglas as they sat at the dinner table in the evening of his return from a brief trip to Brussels. "I've taken a job at the European Common Market headquarters in Brussels and I start in two weeks," he continued. Although the United States was not a member of the Common Market, Douglas's international journalistic experience made him an interesting candidate for the newly expanding organization, where officials were eager to build commercial ties with the United States, and because of the UK's recent entry into the Market, English speakers were in high demand.

"That sounds exciting! If you're starting in two weeks, there's not much time to get things moving here."

"Well, that's where you come in, Thalia! I'm going ahead, and you can sell this house and wind up our affairs here and join me. I'll find us a place to live in Belgium and it will be ready when you get through here."

"Douglas, I'm not sure I can do all that. It's a big job, and on my own...!"

He cut her off in mid-sentence "You can do it! I have perfect faith in your efficiency and competence. A good real estate agent will be able to do most of it, and you can hire packers and shippers."

"No, I don't think you understand. I'm pregnant."

"Oh." Douglas hesitated for a moment before continuing. "How far along are you?"

"Two months."

"Then there's plenty of time. You don't even look pregnant yet. Get rid of it. I think we should go ahead and do it as we planned.

Appalled, Thalia protested, "Douglas, don't you hear me? You are going to be a father again! WE are expecting another child. I will not 'get rid of it'! "

"Well, like it or not, dearest, WE are moving. Unless you want to stay here with the kids. So, better think it over, then call your favorite real estate agent."

Thalia, angry, hurt, and worried about the future, refused to abort the pregnancy, despite Douglas's continued pressure. "I won't do that, Douglas. There is no reason why we can't have another child. I thought you wanted a family?"

"I do, but it's too soon, and not the right time. We should wait. I want you to take care of the move to Brussels, and if you insist on carrying this pregnancy through, I can't help you."

Thalia, feeling hurt and angry, with the usual resonant twinge of resentment at Douglas and powerless to stop this plan from continuing, did what he ordered but having learned something about her husband and also about money, took some self-protective steps. Douglas meanwhile flew off to Brussels and, although yelping at the cost, was forced to make the necessary funds plus a generous estimate of expenses yet to come available to her in a bank account in her name only. It was not yet legal in the United States for married women to have personal bank accounts or credit cards to handle financial matters in their own names unless they had the consent of their husbands. Now, under pressure to complete the move, Douglas provided such a letter to permit Thalia to have an account because of his absence from the United States and the need for her to manage the family's financial affairs during his absence.

She obtained both a bank account and a credit card and entrusted the sale of the little Alexandria house to a stylish young woman who claimed the most exclusive clientele in the real estate business in the area and a shockingly high sales commission, while Thalia interviewed movers and packers and engaged the highest bidders on these jobs. Satisfied that this move would be exceedingly expensive for Douglas, she sat back to wait for results.

Then, a truly astonishing development, a sizzling bolt of literary lightning, brought Douglas hotfooting back across the Atlantic. The New York magazine, The Cultivated Reader, one of the most respected literary publications in the English-speaking world, published a chapter from a lengthy novel called A Family's Pain, by a previously unknown author, Douglas J. Barton. This chapter caused a sensation among critics and readers, and the book was rapidly purchased by a large international publisher for a six-figure advance and, of course, a commission on future sales. Douglas was present at the press presentations of the novel, bowing, signing and smiling to enthusiastic reviews before returning to Brussels, while Thalia remained in Alexandria, having not yet seen a copy of the article.

When did Douglas have time to write a novel, she wondered, and how could he have done this without my knowing anything about it? Was he deliberately silent on the topic, or was I too preoccupied with my own life to have noticed? Was he somewhere writing furiously when I suspected he was making love with Beryl the London sparrow? I am so sorry I didn't realize that he really was working too hard, and I wasn't sufficiently supportive. No wonder his feelings for me changed! I must make it up to him, show him that I love him and that I am proud of him for this magnificent creative work.

Like Emma Bovary, the heroine of Flaubert's Madame Bovary, Thalia now fell passionately in love with her husband, more deeply than she had ever been in the past, after he appeared to have engineered a major professional victory. In the novel, Emma, ecstatic at the attention her husband was receiving from the French medical authorities and the public, swore that she would never doubt her husband and would love and support him forever. Thalia had never read Madame Bovary but she reacted in the same fashion as this literary figure to the news of his victory, and pledged her unwavering love and support for him. She did not, however, change any of the financial arrangements she had made.

Then she obtained a copy of the issue of The Cultivated Reader which contained the piece. She immediately understood how Douglas appeared to have achieved a miracle and published a lengthy novel without engaging in long hours of toil. Running to the place where she kept her treasured things, she pulled out the manuscript she had preserved so carefully--Peter's book--and quickly found the chapter in which the author describes the pain of parents whose youngest son, drafted and sent to Vietnam, deserts his unit and flees. He is arrested when he returns to the United States and is sentenced to trial as a deserter. The shame is intolerable to his parents--

how to cope with this disgrace, they wonder. The very same chapter had been published under Douglas's name in The Cultivated Reader.

Thalia immediately understood the reaction of the parents: she too was shamed by the actions of someone close to her. And angered that her husband had plagiarized his brother's book. Douglas had stolen Peter's work, his life's achievement, and betrayed his brother's memory for money and a moment in the world's spotlight. Thalia didn't know whether or not Peter had tried to publish his book, nor whether he had mentioned the existence of the manuscript in his will, in which he had left all his property to his parents. If he had, of course, it would mean that Douglas had knowingly stolen the work and its potential proceeds from their parents, to whom it legally belonged following Peter's death.

Is there anything I can do, thought Thalia. Call an attorney, contact the publishers, tell someone at the magazine? There is one thing I must do though to protect the children and me, and that is to make sure my copy of the manuscript is safe. I wonder if Douglas's letter of permission for me to have my own bank account will allow me to have a safe deposit box. In my name, without allowing Douglas access. A quick phone call to the bank assured her that she could certainly rent a safe deposit box without further permission from her husband, and that she did not have to permit him access. The manuscript was placed in the new box, with only Thalia's name on the access permission. This, she felt, gave her a major bargaining chip in the case of pressure from Douglas on something important--a request for divorce, for example, or maintenance for her and the children in the future. With increasing maturity, she realized the need to ensure her own financial security.

The house was sold two months later, and Thalia, her pregnancy now obvious, moved with Daniel to a hotel for the final week while the sale was finalized and the packing done. The accounts were settled, and she had made a substantial profit on the sale of the house, which would more than cover the costs of packing and shipping their household goods to Belgium. No word had come from Douglas of any plans for their residence in Brussels, and in a phone call, expensive but, she felt, necessary, she asked him for information about an address to which their household effects could be shipped. He replied casually that he had not had time to find a place where they would live, and that she should place their things in storage and come ahead. Something, he said, would work out eventually.

With misgivings, Thalia did as he directed but she decided that she would visit London on the way to Brussels, so that she could see her friends from *Oriana*, and made plans to allow her and Daniel to spend a few days in London. Although there was plenty of money in her own bank account, she asked Douglas to send additional funds, saying that her pregnancy and her hard work on the sale of the house and packing made some leisure time necessary for her. She could, she said, stay with her friends Dorrie and John Ridd at their sprawling property in Surrey, close to London, where they raised children and bred racehorses, commuting by air back and forth to New Zealand where John still maintained Doone Valley Farm.

Douglas reluctantly complied and sent the funds requested; Thalia made plans with Dorrie and John for their visit. She and Daniel arrived in London by air on a golden late summer morning, and were driven to Surrey through the enchantment of the English countryside, so familiar and beloved to Australians from their reading of so much English literature. Surely, she thought, things will go better with Douglas now that I am in a place that means so much to me.

Chapter Sixteen
To London and Beyond

And so it was done. Thalia left the United States, taking with her the memories of those seven years--the friends, the home she and Douglas had shared, the experiences, but little else--only the child in her womb, her son Daniel, a few belongings, and a slowly disintegrating marriage. Not exploding in rage and flames--they were too civilized or perhaps too indifferent for that, but dissolving in the bile of unexpressed sadness and resentment.

Thalia was beginning to realize that she had misread Douglas in the beginning, that what she had seen as his strength and drive was really his desire for control of his environment, in which she was included. Perhaps, she thought, I wasn't old enough to make good judgments. And I didn't expect his treachery in his dealings with his brother's work. We have been married for seven years, and now I am not sure I can stay in this marriage. With this pregnancy this is not the time to make a decision, but I must think about everything. Perhaps when we get settled in Brussels, I will have a chance to think and plan.

But then there was London! Ahhh, London! Light, gaiety, fun, a renewal of youth, and fabulous shopping. Dorrie and John were delightful companions, and Daniel slotted happily into the Ridd household of children and pets, leaving Thalia free to indulge herself. She moved to the Connaught Hotel for a few days, recommended by Dorrie and paid for by Douglas's money in her bank account, and renewed her friendship with the theatre group, all of whom, with the exception of Nigel, were happily performing in Shaftesbury Avenue drawing room comedies. "Such a relief, darling," said Charmian, "to be back in the civilized world after a year in the outer darkness of Australia!" Thalia agreed politely, although inwardly she resented this description of her homeland.

It appeared that Nigel, absent from London, was working in the north of England on a new play by an *avant garde* playwright which it was hoped would move to a London theatre later in the season. He had acquired a small reputation in contemporary circles for his previous work in repertory theatre, and according to Julian was regarded by London producers as a promising talent but not yet widely enough known by theatregoers that he could carry the weight of important new productions.

Having wanted very much to see Nigel, Thalia was disappointed by his absence. She quizzed Charmian and Julian about his off-stage activities, and learned from Charmian that he sometimes had a girlfriend. "Are they sleeping together?" inquired Thalia, feeling resentful that Nigel hadn't sworn lifetime celibacy after her refusal of him but then, realizing that this was a little unreasonable of her, hurried to say, "Well, I hope he's happy anyway."

Charmian replied, "I don't know about the sleeping arrangements, but I'll ask Amelia. She always knows things like that. As for happiness, I think he is quite focused on making a brilliant career for himself, and I believe he has a good chance."

Amelia of course had felt it was her responsibility to let Nigel know that Thalia was in town—any opportunity to exacerbate a potential problem was golden for Amelia--and that she had been inquiring about him, and on Sunday morning Nigel himself arrived at the Connaught, having driven five hours from York, leaving after Saturday night's performance and not needed again until Monday night's show. He phoned from the foyer, saying, "Thalia! Why didn't you tell me you were coming? I would have been here earlier! How long are you staying? Have lunch with me! And dinner!"

"We're leaving for Brussels tomorrow on the train, about 10 in the morning, but I have to go back to Dorrie and John's place today to get Daniel, so you and I can have lunch but not dinner. I am glad you came up though—I would hate to have missed you! This is my first time in London, and I would like you to be my guide."

"We can have lunch at The Ivy! It's Sunday, so there won't be many names there, but next time we'll go after my show, and see who shows up. Maybe I will be the big name by then. But who's Daniel? I thought his name's Douglas."

"Daniel's my son. He's four. He's mingling with Dorrie and John's flock right now and having a lot of fun, but tomorrow we are off to join Douglas in Brussels. We're going to be living there, so I'll be back in London often."

"May I come up to your room, so that we can talk? I didn't know you had a son."

"No, you can't come up, and yes, I have a son. I'll be down in about half an hour, and we can talk then. I need to dress and pack. I'm sure the Connaught will give you a lovely cuppa and a biscuit, or more probably a full British breakfast in the Grill."

"I thought you were anxious to see me!"

"Not that anxious." Thalia said, laughing, "I'll be down soon."

In her luxurious room overlooking Carlos Place in Mayfair, Thalia dressed and packed, leaving her suitcase by the door. She would ask for it to be brought down when she paid the bill and checked out; I wonder what this will cost Douglas, she mused. Well, certainly with the stolen wealth from his brother's book, Douglas could afford this famous London hotel. In the meantime, there was Nigel waiting downstairs for her and a London full of possibilities. Is it true, she wondered, what Samuel Johnson said, "*when a man is tired of London, he is tired of life; for there is in London all that life can afford."*

For Thalia, one of the delights of the Connaught was the staircase which led from the foyer to the guest rooms, installed in the early twentieth century during the modernization of the old hotel. Lit by a glass dome, its carved oak railings shone with the care and polishing of almost a hundred years, while its modern carpet with its geometric stripes edged by deep pink borders hushed the sound of footsteps and harmonized with the large traditional vases of pink and blue hydrangeas which stood at its foot in the foyer. Located in the Mayfair district just off New Bond Street, she enjoyed the history of the hotel and how, although relatively new in London's measure of existence, it reflected so much of the city's past. Named for Queen Victoria's seventh child Arthur, Duke of Connaught and Strathearn, it had hosted queens and commoners, politicians and honest men. French President General Charles de Gaulle had lived there in exile during World War II, during which time he is said to have participated in the planning for the D-Day landings. The hotel's story continued and London changed around it, changing but never losing the accretion of memories from its long past.

As she descended the stairs, she could see Nigel waiting for her while he watched the comings and goings of the guests in the foyer. She thought how much he had matured since she had seen him last, and how attractive she found him now. He stood up when he saw her on the stairs, and she noticed the elegance with which he carried his height and how handsome his maturing face. Did I miss all this on board *Oriana,* she wondered. I thought he was just a kid like me, green and silly, and I didn't take him seriously. I wish I had.

"Thalia! I thought I would never see you again after Vancouver, but here you are!" Coming closer, he moved as if to embrace her but stopped, apparently disconcerted by something. Then, very quietly, "You... are you pregnant?"

She laughed. "No, Nigel. I have been eating too well in England! Of course I am, you silly. It happens, you know, to married women."

"Oh, I wasn't ready for this."

He looked stricken, and although she couldn't imagine why her pregnancy should provoke this reaction, instinctively Thalia tried to help him. "I'm sorry. I thought someone would have told you." Thinking a joke might help to ease the stress he seemed to feel, she said "Amelia's claws must need sharpening—I can't imagine how she failed to pass along this little snippet."

Evidently making an effort to compose himself, he laughed a little and said, "Well, she's getting older, like all of us."

Puzzled by his evident distress at the sight of her pregnancy, Thalia went to the desk to leave her key, and asked the clerk on duty to have her bill prepared for her return. Surely he might have expected something like this, she thought--she was, after all, married and of prime age for building a family. Then, turning to Nigel, she said happily "Let's go! Show me this wonderful London! I am ready to fall in love." He offered her his arm, and together they walked out of the hotel, smiling at the two imposing doormen outside the entrance.

"Taxi, please," said Nigel to one of the men, who blew his whistle for a cab. A traditional London taxi, black by law and custom, pulled up sedately to the door. Thalia was able to enter the roomy vehicle without bending her head, while Nigel needed to incline his head just a little. Traditionally, the cabs were sufficiently high to permit a man wearing a bowler hat to ride in the back seat while still wearing his hat, uncrushed and untouched by contact with the vehicle's frame. "The Ivy," he said to the driver.

Orright, guv." said the driver as he pulled into the quiet Sunday traffic on Mount Street and headed toward New Bond Street.

Delighted by this first meeting with one of the traditions of the city, Thalia laughed softly. "I love that it hasn't changed in a hundred years! That it's still the same as in so many novels and stories of London! I hope it will stay the same forever!"

Nigel turned to her, and without words, took her hand and kissed it gently before returning it to her, but then grasped it tightly for the remainder of the ride. She tried once to remove it from his grip, but he held on. She sighed, then said, "Nigel, this is a bad idea. I'm still married."

"...'still'?" That implies that you are considering making a change."

Thalia didn't answer.

"The Ivy, guv," said the driver. "Tha'll be two and thrupence."

Nigel paid and they stepped onto the street in front of The Ivy, a longtime traditional restaurant much patronized by theatre people. "So, Thalia, when I get to be a success, this is where we'll come after the opening night of my show, and people will applaud as you and I walk in together, and I'll wave and look modest, and you will look gorgeous, all dressed up, and beaming with pride in me! And we'll eat roast beef for our dinner, even though it's eleven o'clock at night."

"I can't take you seriously, Nigel!" said Thalia, laughing. "I'm still married, and I have no intention of changing things. Kindly stop the nonsense."

Grinning, Nigel replied. "I only have today to try again to convince you to leave what's-his-name and run away with me, so you can't blame me for trying! But alright—I'll stop if you let me drive you to Dorrie and John's place this afternoon, and then take you to the train tomorrow. Is it a deal?"

Thalia gave in and agreed to his suggestion and Nigel kept his word. "The Ivy's been here in Covent Garden since 1917 in the middle of the Great War. People didn't go to the theatre in blue jeans and shabby clothes in those days for a first night or a royal command performance, they wore evening clothes and looked as grand as possible. Then they'd come out of the show, and say, 'Let's have supper at The Ivy', and they'd come swanning in here, hoping to see the stars of the show or a royal or two, and they still do."

On the drive down to Doone Haven Stables, they talked easily, remembering incidents from the voyage across the Pacific, Nigel saying again how moved he had been by the sight of the albatross which had followed the ship for so long. “So big a bird, but so small a creature in relation to the ocean yet such a master of its environment, surviving the adversity of wind and rain, cyclonic storms, and sometimes times of doldrums with no wind to assist its flight. It symbolized freedom to me, still does, you know.”

At the gate to the property, he pulled the car to the side for a moment and turned to Thalia, saying, “I want you to know.... “He stopped, drew a deep breath, then continued “I wish this baby...” gesturing to her obvious pregnancy, “were mine.” Then, he started the car again and pulled up to the door, where a glorious rabble of children, dogs and people surged out in joyous welcome.

Chapter Seventeen

Brussels

Thalia opened the conversation with Dorrie that evening, "Dorrie, Nigel wants to take Daniel and me to the boat train in London. Ummm—I don't feel comfortable with it. Do you think you could take us?"

Dorrie laughed. "Is he flirting again? He doesn't give up easily, I'll say that for him. Of course! No worries, but we can do better than that—we'll take John's big car and all the kids and dogs, and take you to Dover. It really isn't much further than London, and it's pretty country. I'll break it to Nigel in the morning."

But she forgot to break it to Nigel, who was spending the night in her house, so he was unprepared for the jolly caravan that greeted him outside the front door at the appointed time. "You can ride with us and we'll bring you back here, Nigel, or you can drive your car if you prefer to go alone and meet us at the wharf, your pick. Thalia's riding with me," said Dorrie. Nigel, although surprised and a little daunted by the merry commotion, chose to ride with the group, and Dorrie busied herself assigning places in the vehicle. "I'm the driver, and Thalia, you can ride in front with me. Nigel, you're in the back seat with the baby, and you can also keep order among the boys in the way-back with the dogs. The Irish wolfhound and the borzoi are too big to fit in and they squabble with each other, so they can't come." When did sweet ladylike Dorrie become so bossy, Thalia wondered.

Nigel, realizing that he had been outgunned by Dorrie's generalship of her junior and four-legged cavalry, accepted his defeat graciously and took his assigned seat, although not without an eyeroll for Thalia. An outburst of growling and yipping broke out in the way-back and Dorrie, patience wearing thin, shouted "I told you, children! Get those two out NOW!" The culprits were removed and peace broke out, while the adults seated themselves, luggage in the back seat with Nigel and the baby, and began Thalia and Daniel's journey to their new home, new country, new continent.

"Is Douglas meeting you at Ostend?" asked Dorrie.

"No, we'll take the train from Ostend to Brussels. He says he doesn't have time to make the drive to the coast," Thalia replied, "but Danny's never been on a train, so I think he'll enjoy that anyway. It's not long— just about an hour and a half." Laughing, she said, "I can't get used to how short the distances are here! Everything seems so close — you can go from one country to another faster than we can go from one state to another in the US or Australia!"

They left the narrow country lanes overhung with briar rose and honeysuckle too quickly for Thalia, and soon their car joined the motorway from London to Dover, speeding with trucks and large vehicles in the morning traffic. On arrival in Dover, Dorrie navigated efficiently to the ferry terminal where the auto ferry was waiting. Foot passengers were embarking rapidly, with auto traffic moving aboard more slowly. They made their farewells quickly, Nigel showing a desire to linger and perhaps hug Thalia, but Dorrie moved him along with a "Hurry up, Nigel! I've got to get the car out of here!", and at last the big car moved majestically away, small hands and dogs' tails waving from the way-back.

The voyage would take no more than two hours, and Thalia chose seats inside the cabin for them, thinking that if the weather were pleasant, they could go out on deck once the vessel cleared the harbor mole in Dover. She hoped to see the fabled "white cliffs of Dover", so emblematic of the courage of the British nation during World War II.

All the vehicles had been loaded onto the ferry now, and the watertight doors to the vehicle decks closed with loud bangs as the powerful engines began to move the craft away from the wharf. The ferry was docked at the wharf closest to the entrance in the long stone wall, the "mole", which protected the harbor from the open water of the Channel, so the vessel was quickly outside in open water. “Let’s go out on deck, Danny, and see the waves,” said Thalia, and they walked through the doors onto the deck.

The sea was calm, and seagulls followed the ship; Daniel laughed and clapped his hands when he saw the birds. “Can we feed them, Mummy?” he asked, and Thalia reached into her bag for the stale bread she had saved from breakfast that morning. Walking to the rail she showed him how to position himself with the wind behind him so that the bread would not be blown back onto the ship, and he began to toss pieces to the birds which thronged the water below, squawking and squabbling over the morsels, while Danny squealed with delight.

Thalia stood behind him, enjoying his pleasure in the simple task of feeding birds, and remembering another bird, the wandering albatross, that had followed *Oriana*, and had led to her meeting Nigel for the first time. As she stood there, her eye fell on her hands clasping the white metal rail in front of her, so utilitarian by comparison with the elegance of the polished wood railings on *Oriana*. My hands have changed since then, she thought. They look grownup now—the hands of an adult, a mother, a wife, a person of consequence, with manicured nails, smooth ovals lightly polished, Douglas’s diamond engagement ring and wedding ring on the third finger, left hand, and now gone from the right hand her grandmother’s little silver ring. Soft Irish silver, the Celtic cross, old and a little battered by age and every-day use, she didn't wear it anymore because it seemed like a child's ring, and it waited in her jewelry box for a future daughter. Is the one on the way a daughter? I hope so, but I also hope I know how to raise a daughter.

They were a little beyond mid-Channel now, and today the ancient sea barrier to invasions of England was calm, quiet, with no sign of the stormy weather which had been a protection, and which had sometimes made crossings epically difficult, legendary in travelers' memoirs.

But weather apart, this for me is another consequential sea voyage, she thought, albeit short. The first one ended with my reunion with Douglas and my marriage; what will this one end with--divorce? Will life in Europe please me more than life in the USA? I know it's not the place, it's the marriage. I am pretty sure now that it's wrong for both of us, but I don't yet know what to do. Would talking to Douglas help? Oh, probably not. Not only my hands have changed, mused Thalia—I've changed too, become harder, I think, more judgmental and not kind. Living with Douglas has done that. I need to work on changing back to my old self. If that's still possible.

The ferry had entered the Ostend harbor basin now, and she could see the crowd of people and lines of vehicles gathered on the wharf waiting to board the returning ferry. She and Daniel would need a taxi to take them and their luggage to the railway station. Scanning the wharf to see if there was a taxi rank where she might get one, she was suddenly surprised to see Douglas waiting in the crowd. "There's Daddy! See him down there?" She pointed him out to Daniel, and they both began to wave; Douglas saw them, and waved back, pointing toward the car park. Presumably his new car was waiting there to take them to Brussels.

They tied up and Douglas bounded aboard, in a rush as usual, and trailed by a porter with a handcart; greeting Thalia with a brief hug, he gave Daniel a solemn handshake followed by a noisy laughing scuffle and a hug. "Okay, troops, let's go. Where're the bags?" The porter gathered their luggage, and Douglas led the way from the ferry to the car park, where his new BMW waited. When people and bags were settled, he turned to Thalia and said "We're going to the Hotel Metropole in Brussels, where we have a suite for a short time. You can start house hunting tomorrow." He pulled the car out of the parking area and onto the main road leading to Brussels.

Do I engage, Thalia wondered, or let this go by and discuss it later? How can I hunt for a house when I have no idea what the city looks like, the desirable areas to live, where Douglas works, where to find a nursery school for Daniel, there is so much to learn. But he's in a good mood, so let's not spoil it. "The Metropole? Sounds very grand! Is it in the center of the city?"

"Yes. It's close to the Bourse and the Opera, and the old part of town, where there are a lot of restaurants. The car arrived yesterday, so I decided to surprise you and pick you up, so you didn't have to take the train."

"Thank you! We're a bit tired today. I'll be glad to get settled."

"How was London?"

"Oh, alright. A bit dull, really. Nothing interesting happened."

And so with a lie, Thalia arrived in the country where she would pass the rest of her life. Something interesting *had* happened, something which needed reflection and clarification, not yet ready to be spoken of out loud. And perhaps there was some hope of change, she thought, hidden behind the dark uncertainties that presented themselves in the current state of her marriage.

Chapter Eighteen
Hotel Metropole, Brussels

The suite in the Metropole was quiet, mostly because it faced onto an interior light well of the hotel and had no view of anything but other windows and a little slice of sky four floors above. It was dowdy but comfortable, in a heavy, old-fashioned style of big overstuffed chairs and sofas with slightly worn velvet upholstery crowding the space, elaborate window draperies, and wall-to-wall carpeting with flowery designs. The suite consisted of a bedroom, a sitting room, and a bathroom, with a folding bed in the sitting room for Daniel, and a double bed for Thalia and Douglas in the bedroom.

Adequate for a short time, Thalia thought, but she would certainly be looking for something larger and more modern, available as soon as possible. The hotel's public rooms were large and grand, with imposing furniture in the Art Deco style and food in the substantial nineteenth-century French manner. Daniel found the elevator enchanting, with its enclosing web of gilded metal and its accordion doors, all encircled by the marble staircase which led to the major areas of the hotel. He discovered the joy of sliding down the shiny brass handrails from floor to floor, hoping to beat Thalia in the elevator to the ground floor.

Douglas continued to insist that the search for a home was Thalia's responsibility, saying, "Thalia, I have to work. It's up to you now to find a suitable place."

"Douglas, I don't speak French at all! And I need to take care of Daniel."

"Hotel has babysitters, Thalia. You can pay for one sometimes. And I don't speak French either. So, get on with it and stop complaining." He jotted down a couple of suggestions for suburban locations which might be suitable, and called down to the desk and ordered a copy of *Le Monde*, the Brussels daily newspaper, to be sent up.

At first angry and resentful, as she had become in most of her dealings with Douglas, Thalia gradually accepted the task, thinking that at least she was in Europe now. She and Daniel took a walk to a nearby department store where she was able to buy an English/French dictionary, as well as a green Michelin guide to Brussels and Its environs, and she returned to the hotel feeling somewhat equipped for the task ahead.

She applied herself to the English/French dictionary, and also to *Le Monde*. A classified ad caught her eye in "*Maisons à Louer*"--*Une maison bijou! charmante, dans un lieu tres joli, auprès de la ville et*........"

“A jewel of a house, charming, in a pretty location, close to the city and.....” So, she challenged the pre-war telephone system of the Hotel Metropole and succeeded in reaching the agency. “I am sorry, I don’t speak French. Do you speak English?”

“Certainly, Madame. We have many *clientes Anglaises*. How can we help you?”

A brief explanation from Thalia, and, “*Ah, oui, la maison à Boitsfort, madame. C’est charmante*... We can show it to you today”.

An appointment time was established, a hotel babysitter was engaged, a lively young woman picked Thalia up at the hotel in her tiny French car, and they were off. Wildly. The wrong way down one-way streets, two-wheel right turns, fast and faster through the narrow cobblestoned streets of the old quarter of the town, trailing a stream of machine-gun French from the driver and vile imprecations from taxi drivers and pedestrians. No honking was permitted in Brussels Thalia had learned, so there was a fine selection of oaths, gestures and light flashing reserved for errant motorists. As her terror subsided, she began to think--look at me! Riding in this tiny European car with this sophisticated young woman, speaking French! Well, she is speaking it, I am just smiling and nodding.

The *petit bijou* was a tall brick house with a red tile roof, on the side of a steep hill with thirty-two stone steps up to the front door. The little vestibule led to an entrance hall with black and white marble tiles, a grey-carpeted staircase to the left, a two-level salon to the right. Giant pink roses blushed on the wallpaper in the hall and up the stairs, oatmeal-textured wallpaper in the salon. Straight ahead was the kitchen, with yellow daisy wallpaper cheerfully clashing with the rosiness of the hall, and one lone cabinet. Beyond the kitchen was the scullery, with a small stainless steel sink and draining board. As was usual in European rental houses, there were no appliances, almost no cabinets, and only bare electric wires protruding from the ceilings where light fixtures should be. "*Ça, c'est normal*", said her escort.

The house ascended like a Christmas tree, each room with its floor two or three steps higher than the preceding one. There were three large bedrooms, each on a different level, and one smaller attic room high above, which Mlle Florence (she and Thalia were on first-name terms by now) pointed out would be a perfect bedroom for an *au pair,* and eleven levels total, including the *cave* and the *grenier*—the cellar and attic. Thalia was enchanted. She wanted this house.

Douglas refused to participate in the negotiations with the owner's representative, an older Belgian woman, an artist, beaded, beshawled, and determined to carry out her son's wishes to the ultimate degree. "*Non.*" she said firmly "*Mon fils* says no to diplomatic clause," a kick-out provision commonly used by foreigners who might be transferred elsewhere at short notice. "He say I must say *Non*." Thalia offered more money. "*Non*." She swore they (well, she) would take good care of the house. "*Non!*" Replant the garden? Re-wallpaper the salon? *"Non, non, non.*"

At last, Thalia, her eyes filled with tears, pleaded on behalf of her unborn baby. "I have a little boy, and now a new baby soon to arrive, and no home for them!"

"Oof..." huffed Madame Rennes. "Mon Dieu! I cannot refuse such a request. *D'accord--vous l'avez, clauses diplomatiques et tout! Mon fils va me tuer!*" But her son didn't kill her, and all was arranged amicably from then on. She invited Thalia and Douglas to her next *vernissage,* the ceremonial varnishing of a new painting, explaining that very little actual varnishing took place and that the occasion would be purely social, and that she would be delighted to introduce them into her social circle.

Before Thalia and Douglas could move in, Thalia had to take care of the most important ritual of renting a house in Europe — the "*etat de lieu*", the state of the premises. An inspector sent by the owner inspected the house in great detail, listing such things as a place where wallpaper had been gondola-ed over a corner (i.e., not properly cut to fit but bent, leaving space behind it), a crack in the glass in a bedroom window, or scrapes on the parquet floor in the salon. The color of the paint on the walls, the wear on the carpet, descriptions of roses and daisies and oatmeal on the wallpapers—all recorded in a legal document which would be preserved by the owner, with a copy for the tenant, and produced when they left and checked again for damage done, with little allowance for the scrapes and marks of daily life.

Thalia did it all, with minimum help from Douglas. At last, *etat de lieu* in hand, she announced triumphantly to Douglas that they could move out of the Metropole, and occupy their own house! Number 25 Avenue des Rosiers, Watermael Boitsfort, the charming house on the pretty street lined with *rosiers*, the rosebushes for which it was named, waited for them!

Their furniture was delivered from the storage facility, and all the unpacking was done by the movers, Thalia purchased kitchen cabinets, refrigerator, washer, dryer and stove, a plumber was engaged to install them--"*Oolala*!" he said *"C'est un usine*!" (It's a factory!), and the family moved in.

Douglas blew into the house some days later on a gust of cold wind and rustling leaves, saying, "Thalia, those steps out front are going to be tiring for you to get the groceries up, and the baby stuff too." Then seeing her teacup, "Glass of wine for me? But the house looks good! Let's go out for dinner! I've got news!"

"Douglas, I'm too tired! And so's Danny. Let's stay here and I'll make us some soup and an omelette, while you tell us your news."

"OK. Sounds good. I'm being sent to Paris!"

"But… we've just got into this house!"

"Oh, it's a temporary assignment. A month at most, maybe. I'll be staying in a hotel, and will able to come home on weekends, and you can come down there for weekends too, after the baby comes. Exciting, yes?"

"But… what about the baby? It's only two months now. Can you make sure you will be here for that?"

"I'll try, Thalia, but you'll have the *au pair* and we'll get the midwife set up in advance. If I'm not here, I'm sure everything will be fine. But I promise I will try"

And with that, he drained his glass and went upstairs to see how Thalia had arranged his clothes and personal things.

Chapter Nineteen
Eavesdropping

Thalia was early for the afternoon tea given by the wife of the U.S. ambassador to Belgium in the grand house on Avenue Winston Churchill. Leaving her coat with the attendant on the *rez de chausée*, the street floor, she went upstairs to the solarium below the glass dome to find a comfortable chair in which to wait and rest. Lovely, she thought, to just be quiet for a while in such a beautiful room. I am tired of this pregnancy; it seems to have gone on for a year. It's time it ended. I would like to be slim again, and be able to wear pretty clothes, not these lumpy maternity garments. Almost there now though, just a week or two more. And Douglas will be back for the birth, of course. That will be good, he's been away for months. I had no idea the temporary duties in Paris would last for so long.

She heard the street door opening below, and amid the chatter of greeting, feminine voices floated clearly up to her. "Well, do you think he'll come back from Paris when the baby arrives?" said a voice with a British accent. A French-accented voice replied, "*Alors! Ça depende*--if Clemence doesn't want him to leave her, I think he'll stay there." Another voice joined the vocal tapestry, this time American, sweetly drawling, "Y'all, She seems to like his... attentions, and if she wants to keep playing, I think he's more than willin'." The door opened again, she could hear a jumble of voices, now the brittle ice of British upper-class English against the hissing sibilance of French, interwoven with the attendant's heavier Spanish-accented French. Suddenly one voice rang through with crystal clarity--"Do you think Thalia knows?" And then, another voice, "He is obsessed with Clemence, my dears! I hear he plans to divorce...".

Thalia's vision darkened and no more sounds reached her... they are talking about Douglas. She felt cold, so cold she thought she must have died, but in her ears she could hear her blood pounding as her heart worked to keep her and her unborn child alive. What shall I do, she asked herself. How did I not know this? Have I been blind? Were the signs there and I missed them? Not only my husband's unfaithfulness, but the cruelty of those I thought were my friends! Who is Clemence? Have I met her?

The first of the women were mounting the staircase; seeing her, they greeted her smilingly as if nothing had been said. Her years of dealing with Douglas's rudeness and careless treatment of people sustained her. His training of her had been effective, she realized. She knew how to save her face--he had given her enough practice. Struggling out of the so-comfortable low chair, she straightened her back and walked to the wrought-iron railing surrounding the solarium and the staircase and said, "How nice to see you all and hear your voices. I am afraid I can't stay for tea. I must go to Avenue Louise to shop for the baby. I hope Mrs. Butterworth will forgive me for leaving without seeing her." Carrying herself as lightly as possible and with all the dignity her pride could find, she descended the stairs. "*Mon manteau, s'il vous plait, Madame*," she said to the attendant. Some of the women still in the entrance hall tried to smooth over the situation, but Thalia didn't respond to them and left, as the attendant said softly, "*Bonne journée, Madame*".

Outside in the wet-mop greyness of a Belgian autumn afternoon, she hailed a cab and told the driver to take her for a half-hour drive through the *Forêt de Soignes*, then to Avenue Louise to shop. The forest, a remnant of the ancient Saonian beech forest, still formed an impressive green belt to the south of Brussels. Beech trees contain a substance in their roots which discourages other plants from growing under them, and the ground beneath the gray trunks was mostly clear of underbrush. The trees grew straight and tall, and to Thalia they resembled the aisles of Gothic cathedrals, the trees standing like columns, and the branches arching gracefully high above.

She was tense and preoccupied as the cab moved slowly along the small roads twisting through the trees, passing gloomy ponds of black water filled with floating dead leaves. Here and there, old wayside shrines which had once served to reassure travelers fearful of the mysterious mischief and evil of the forest spirits still stood in picturesque semi-ruin. As the taxi passed the macabrely-named "Pond of the Drowned Children", she wondered who were the "drowned children", who drowned them, and why? Were they once warm living beings, or just lurid figments of the medieval imagination? In her mind, she heard Douglas's words "get rid of it!" Could this baby have been one of the "drowned children" if she had agreed? It was no wonder the people of other ages had feared deep forests like this.

How could she have been so blind about Douglas? Who is Clemence? How long had this been going on? As she searched her memory, she recalled little things in the past, seemingly insignificant things, perhaps small signposts of what was ahead. And she recalled too seeing a striking woman across the room at one of the many formal receptions to which she and Douglas had been invited when they first arrived. An acquaintance had identified her to Thalia as Madame Laulan, the wife of Pierre Laulan, the chief of section for whom Douglas would be working. Douglas had abandoned Thalia in a corner at the reception, and she had been too overwhelmed by this new milieu to dare to introduce herself, but she had been impressed by the beauty and confidence of this woman across the room, with her upswept blonde hair and expensively chic clothing.

Oh, yes, I think he has been unfaithful before, possibly many times. This Madame Laulan doesn't seem his type though--too refined, subtle, elegant. I thought his type was Beryl, the girl in the theatre group in DC. I wondered about her at the time, and there were others, but I blotted out my doubts so that I could continue my comfortable life. But now, I have to face them.

The new baby was first among her considerations. Could she depend on Douglas for support for her and two children? Was the story about Clemence and his desire for a divorce true, or a snatch of spiteful speculation? And how should she deal with this whole thing? Is there anyone who could advise me, she wondered. Well, to begin with, I am going to make sure he feels it in his pocket, where he is most sensitive. And I think I will go to visit friends in London; Douglas will have to take care of things here for a while. I can stay with Dorrie and John, and perhaps Dorrie and Charmian can give me advice.

The cab had left the forest roads now and was on Boulevard du Souverain, heading for the inner ring road and Avenue Louise, the city's most elegant shopping street. "Please take me to Maison Gregoire," Thalia said. Gregoire, the premier couturier in Brussels, would have everything she wanted, at a price which would, she hoped, make Douglas blink. And from there, she would go to Du Bateau, children's equipment from Paris,

London and New York, certain to be able to assist with the blinking.

The cab pulled up outside a building in the Belgian *art nouveau* style, once a private mansion but now the atelier of the couturier Armand Gregoire, a favorite with the wives of the many international expatriates of the city. Brussels, with its long history of occupation, and now the headquarters of numerous international organizations and corporations, survived World War II relatively unscathed to become one of the most fashionable cities in Europe, its elegant shops and restaurants catering to a wealthy and discriminating population.

Thalia asked the cab driver to wait for her. I am not going to take the bus home, she thought, Douglas will just have to pay for this too. The receptionist greeted her and directed her to the elevator which would take her to the showroom on the first floor where a *vendeuse* would be assigned to her, to help her make her choices and send them to her home. *"Bonjour, madame. Puis-je vous aider?"* asked the slim, elegant young woman who met her as she stepped out of the little *ascenseur* painted to resemble the beribboned boxes of chocolate in which the city specialized.

Thalia replied in French, but found herself quickly out of her depth in that language and switched to English. "I would like to buy some new things to wear for a trip after my *accouchement*. A couple of summer dresses, a bathing suit, and some lingerie."

"Madame is taking a voyage, a trip to somewhere sunny, perhaps a hotel on the Côte d'Azur? Or a villa in Corsica or Sardinia, where the royal family goes?"

"Yes. Perhaps any of those, or maybe Casablanca, or Tangiers... or, who knows? I need pretty things to wear, pretty sexy things!"

"Aaah, Monsieur is happy about the new baby--a son, perhaps?"

Thalia laughed. "Oh, Monsieur already has a son so he is content. This trip is to be a surprise for him." Yes, it surely will be a surprise for Douglas, if he ever learns about it, she thought. "So, show me your most charming things today. *A la mode d'aujourd'hui*. The prices don't matter!"

The two young women had a fine time. Thalia developed her plan for revenge, presenting it as a delightful journey to an exotic place with a beloved man, and the young *vendeuse* innocently entered into it. Together they chose several brilliantly-colored silk dresses, some long full trousers--the *vendeuse* called them "palazzo pantalons"--and suggested low-cut tops to wear with them, and a selection of bare sandals trimmed with gold and silver.

The lingerie of a couture house astonished Thalia. She had become accustomed to buying such things in the Monoprix store, and had never imagined such beautiful intimate clothing. Peignoirs and robes of silk georgette, falling softly from translucent lace bodices artfully hinting at the body beneath, smooth, sculptured, satin slips to wear beneath formal afternoon dresses, lacy slips and combinations, robes of silk taffeta in delicate shades, wrapping the breasts into silk packages above rustling skirts, discreetly tempting but modest— "*Quand les domestiques sont présent*, *Madame*" said her helper. Madame made her choices, gave Douglas's bank information to the floor manager, and arranged for all to be delivered to her home the next day, COD as was customary. When it arrived, she would write a check for it and he would learn about it when he checked the household accounts next month. She wanted to be there when he did that.

Smiling, she exited the house, her mood much improved since her departure from the afternoon tea. The cab took her next to Du Bateau, where she placed an order for toys and clothes for her son and baby equipment for the new child, to be delivered COD to the quaint house in Watermael Boitsfort, on the edge of the *Forêt.* DuBateau's reputation as an expensive place to shop was fully realized, and Thalia was pleased to think of the effect of the bill on Douglas.

Again the cab was waiting, and this time she directed the driver to take her home. Cecile the *au pair* was at the house, and toddler Daniel was happy to see his mother. They had tea, and about eight o'clock she felt the first pains of labor. She telephoned Douglas in Paris. He was not in his hotel, she learned. The midwife came when Thalia called, and her second child, Minerva, was born around midnight--an easy birth without complications, and a perfect baby.

All told, a successful day, thought Thalia as she rested with her new daughter alongside her. The new baby had arrived safely, and a plan for the future had begun to be devised. Douglas would learn to regret his absence from Minerva's birth.

Chapter Twenty

Unforgivable

The phone line from Paris was not a good connection, but Thalia could hear clearly Douglas's self-justification. "No, Douglas. I do not HAVE to understand! You weren't here for Minerva's birth. You let me down. I will never forgive you."

Muttering, at the other end of the line, "Thalia, I am so so sorry! What can I say... it was an important late meeting, please try to understand!"

She cut him off. "Douglas, I just don't care about your lies. I am through. I heard about Clemence. Apparently everyone in Brussels is talking about it, and they think I'm a fool, a deceived wife. How do you think I feel now? You were away in Paris with your mistress while I was delivering your child. And why haven't you made it home yet? The baby came two days ago! Do you know it's a girl? Or is it that you don't care because you didn't want her in the first place. 'Get rid of it' is what you said."

"I can't leave! There's a crisis with the French government, and I really am working! Of course I know it's a girl, and her name's Minerva, and I do care, you must know that. And I don't have a mistress, anyway. I don't have time!"

"Then who is Clemence?"

Douglas lost his temper. "Alright, Thalia. I have a question for *you*. Who is David?".

Silence. Consternation. Thalia's mind was racing. How did he know? Who could have told him? I need time to think. The best defense is a good offense, she thought and parried as best she could: "I asked you first. Who is Clemence?"

"Don't play games with me, Thalia. I am smarter than you."

"Pride goes before a fall, Douglas." Childish, I know, she thought, but so is he. "Clemence isn't important, not really. She was hardly the first. But tell me about A Family's Pain? Did your brother give you the rights to publish it? How much money have you made from it? Your parents--have you shared with them?"

"I wrote that book. It's mine. Peter had nothing to do with it."

"Then how did I get a manuscript copy of it, with his signature as author?"

"Show it to me. I don't believe you. I want to see it. Where is it?"

"I will show it to you only in the presence of witnesses. My attorney and the US consul."

"Oh, don't be so silly. Who is David?"

"After you. Clemence?"

Douglas broke the connection. Breathe, Thalia reminded herself. Deep breaths, long and slow. Were we always so rough with one another? Why can't I just tell him how much his infidelity hurts me? But what do I say about David, when he asks again? And I wonder how much he knows about that. Someone must have told him. Who could it could have been? Why on earth did I feel I needed to do that—for experience? How stupid I was, I realize it now. But hanging up the phone just now shows his weakness too, Douglas is feeling insecure, threatened.

The baby was crying and she picked her up to tend her, feed and comfort her. Holding the warm little bundle, Minnie as Daniel had begun to call her, and trying to calm the frantic infant, Thalia's breathing quieted and her mind became clearer. My task for now is to protect these two children, each of them half mine, half Douglas's. I have to think first of what is best for them before I decide to follow my own needs. Minerva is so upset. I wonder whether she was aware of my anger at Douglas as she lay there near me in her bassinet while I talked to him on the phone? Are children so sensitive to tension and anger in the atmosphere that a baby could sense it, at two days old?

Who could have told Douglas about David? Again she went over it in her mind. The only people who might have told Douglas were her friends from *Oriana*. Dorrie and John? Not very likely--they had been so lost in their own songline that they noticed nothing but each other. Julian? He seems an unlikely gossip, she thought. He keeps his own counsel, and he has his own reasons to be discreet about such things anyway. Charmian? She had shown herself an ally on board ship. That left Amelia, or the English girls. Of course. Amelia, the gossip, the consumer and purveyor of choice morsels, the competitor for masculine attention. How did she get to Douglas though?

Thalia's thoughts were interrupted when Cecile, the *au pair*, entered the room with Daniel, and her attention was diverted from her problems with Douglas. "Mummy, can I hold Minnie?" the little boy asked, gently stroking the baby's head.

Thalia replied, "Yes, when I finish nursing her, in a few minutes. I think she's almost finished now", as the tiny girl began to fall asleep at her breast, and her brother waited impatiently.

“When’s Daddy coming home, Mummy? Cecile said maybe tomorrow. Was that him on the telephone just now? Why didn’t he want to talk to me?”

“Oh, Danny! Cecile’s almost right--he will be here soon, I don’t think he’ll be here tomorrow, but maybe the next day. And he did want to talk to you, but he was really busy at the office. He said he’ll see you here soon.”

To Cecile, she said, “Could you settle Minerva down, please, while I read Danny his story?” and taking her son by the hand, she led him to bed.

Douglas surprised her by arriving home the next day. After a sleepless night with an upset Minerva, Thalia wasn’t prepared to deal with him then. “Douglas, thank you for coming home. Can we talk later? Right now, I need to engage a baby nurse for a month, to help me with the baby, and a cleaning lady to keep this place in order. Do you want to do that or shall I?”

Another surprise for her “Yes, OK--I’ll get a nurse for the baby. I’m sure the office can give me some contacts. And Cecile can do a little tidying till you find a cleaning woman. Call some of your friends--I bet they all have Spanish *bonnes*.”

Really, is he planning to help, thought Thalia cynically, from her immense tiredness. Feeling guilty, I suppose. Well, let's use it. I'm sure he's right about friends having cleaning women. I don't want to call any of the women from that afternoon tea, but there are a couple of people I can call--perhaps Madame Rennes, or Florence. Or that nice American woman, Daphne Rogers, that I met at the nursery school, she mentioned that she has someone. *Et, la voila*, a quick phone call, and the expatriate underground was opened to Thalia by Daphne. Warm congratulations were given on Minerva's birth, an agency was suggested for a nurse, and a friend of Daphne's maid Gloria was looking for a job.

"So happy that Douglas could get away from that big meeting in Paris!" said Daphne. "I saw him getting into a taxi at the Gare du Midi this morning, just got off the train, I suppose. And then I saw Clemence Laulan too--probably been shopping in Paris, Brussels isn't chic enough for her!"

"Oh, I haven't met her," said Thalia, "I saw her once across the room, at a welcoming reception when we first arrived. She looked very attractive." Shopping in Paris indeed, she thought. They came back to Brussels together on the train, I suppose.

"Attractive isn't the word for Clemence!" answered Daphne, settling down happily for a little morning gossip.

"She used to be a mannequin for one of the big houses in Paris before she married Douglas's boss. She's stunning! But I hear she's quite difficult, and they aren't getting along."

"Difficult how?" asked Thalia, trying to conceal both her avid interest in Clemence and her renewed anger at Douglas. His boss's wife!

"Well, *on ne sait jamais*, what goes on in a marriage," said Daphne, chuckling a little, "really, one has no idea! But she's high maintenance for clothes and luxuries, and I'm not sure Monsieur Laulan has a private income to help with that. Couture's really expensive."

"Does she shop at Maison Gregoire?"

"Oh, goodness, no! She's Dior all the way, with a little fling in London sometimes for casual country stuff. And Italy for shoes."

Douglas entered the room. "Thalia, I need to use the phone, please."

She concluded her conversation with Daphne hastily and relinquished the phone to Douglas, after telling him that she had a lot of helpful information, and could give him the name of an agency, so he could engage a nurse quickly. Cecile had taken Daniel out to ride his tricycle in the park, and Thalia went to tend to Minerva, fearing that Douglas would take the opportunity while they were together in the house to raise the question of David and their future; she was not yet ready to discuss it with him. Her plan was still forming, and she needed time to put it into place. Until then, she would refuse to engage.

Before Thalia had a chance to reflect on her possible course of action, she received a letter from her old friend Pam Collins. As yet unmarried, Pam would be visiting Europe for the first time, and wondered if she could stay with Thalia and Douglas and use their house as her headquarters while travelling around. Thalia was overjoyed. She felt that this, her lifelong friend and confidante, was the trusted person she needed right now to advise her on how to proceed with Douglas.

Chapter Twenty-one

Pam's Visit

Leaving Douglas and the nurse in charge of the children, Thalia met Pam at the airport in Amsterdam. Pam, exhausted from the journey--Melbourne-Sydney-Singapore-London-Amsterdam, an endurance test for passengers but gladly undergone to replace the three-week voyage by sea, was uncommunicative at first. Thalia settled her into Douglas's luxurious BMW, more comfortable for a long drive than her own practical VW wagon, and took her to a coffee shop on the bank of the Prinsengracht Canal, where Pam cheered up after some hot Dutch coffee and breakfast, and they began their reunion after the many years apart.

In the soft misty rain common in the Low Countries, they walked a while for Pam to stretch her legs after the cramped conditions of the long journey, admiring the civilized city, its residents walking and biking to work or school, the canals reflecting the grey clouds and the brilliant colors of the flowers on the banks. "How long do you think you'll stay in Europe?" asked Thalia.

"As long as I can afford to," replied Pam. "Since Mum died, I have no-one left in Melbourne and no real reason to stay there. I'm just thinking about what to do with my life now. I wish you were still in Australia though--I miss you!"

During the 3-hour drive to Brussels, Thalia told her a carefully-edited story of her marriage to Douglas, omitting any mention of David Springer. If necessary, she thought, she could tell Pam about it later. Maybe though it would never be necessary.

Pam was satisfactorily horrified by Douglas's neglect of Thalia, his affairs, and his failure to be with her during Minerva's birth, but most of all with his demand that she abort the baby. "You must leave him, Tally. Come home to Australia with the kids, and divorce him. He's not well known there, and a quick, quiet divorce won't cause any scandal; anyhow these days divorce isn't the disgrace it was a couple of years ago. People are much more accepting of it than they used to be, as long as it doesn't get into the papers."

"Pam, it's so far away! And I don't think I can ever be myself, keep growing into an independent person, if I go back. You know my family--all those relatives trying to control me, pulling me in their directions. When I came home for Mum's funeral, they criticized everything--my hair, my clothes, my accent for heaven's sake! Said I sounded like a Yank!" She laughed a little, then, "I do a bit, I guess. Protective coloration, wouldn't you say? Now that Mum's dead, I don't feel that I must go, and I don't think I can do it. And besides... I like living in Europe, I like feeling the history around me, the sophistication of the culture--perhaps someday I can acquire some of that polish, that gloss, and not feel like a provincial in their world."

Pam took a moment to register this, then nodded and said, "I think I understand, and forgive me if you think I'm pushy asking this, but do you and Douglas ever communicate on an emotional level? You seem so alone, so distanced from him in everything you're telling me."

"Interesting, Pam, that you should notice that. I don't think anyone can communicate with Douglas on an emotional level. He guards his feelings and his thoughts, and won't share at all." A long pause, as she navigated the big car through the heavy traffic of the autoroute and thought about how to present the Nigel question to Pam. At last, she said, "and there's something else."

"You have met someone else!" exclaimed Pam. "I knew you wouldn't be happy with Douglas. I told you..."

"How did you guess that? And come on, Pam, don't say, '...told you so'. Nobody ever listens to that--in fact it just makes people more likely to do whatever it is. But yes, I think I have met someone else. I am not yet sure what I am going to do. I have to talk to him."

There, she thought. That's what I need to do. Nigel and I need to talk about this whole thing. Will Douglas give me a divorce or will it be difficult, damaging, for Daniel and Minerva? Does Nigel want to marry me if Douglas and I split up? Do I want to marry Nigel if we divorce? What if I stay with Douglas for the sake of the kids? I've heard of European arrangements like that. Both partners are free to do what they want to do--short-term affairs, or sometimes one stable relationship outside marriage, acknowledged or unacknowledged, publicly or not. Well. I can't tell Pam that I am thinking this, at least not yet. So...

"Almost home! You'll be glad to get a shower and sleep. Nothing to do all day but rest. We're going out to dinner tonight though, just the three of us at the local bistro. Tomorrow we'll go sightseeing, if you'd like to. Brussels is a lovely city."

Too chilly in the evening now to eat under the great chestnut tree in the garden of the bistro, they took a table by the window in the small dining room. *La patronne*, the wife of the owner, greeted them warmly and produced handwritten menus of the evening's offerings. Family-owned, the little café served traditional Belgian dishes such as *carbonnade,* the Flemish-style beef stew made with beer, *waterzooi,* an elaborate chicken soup, and of course *pommes frites*, the staple food of Belgium. The small tables, covered with cobalt-blue Belgian linen cloths, each bore a small candle and a single rose, and the chairs, the traditional Thanet design in curved beechwood, were those seen in almost every traditional bistro in France and Belgium. A simple cheese and dessert cart stood by the entrance, ready to be presented for choices after the main course.

Douglas was at his best that evening. Hale and hearty, mine host--smiling, genial, and engaging. Thalia acknowledged to herself that he was handsome--ice-blue eyes, warm with sympathy now, too often cold of late, tall, broad-shouldered and solid but not heavy, even if there was some suggestion of heaviness in his jaw now as he matured. His manner seemed to indicate that he was fascinated by the conversational offerings of his partner of the moment, Pam, who appeared to be charmed by him, having met him only once, a long time ago in Australia.

“We should all meet up in London,” pronounced Douglas, “I have a friend in theatre there, and if she’s working it would be great for you to meet her, Pam. She does light comedy, musicals, fun stuff, not the heavy stuff Thalia prefers!” A friend in theatre, thought Thalia. Who do you suppose that would be? Could it be Beryl? But thank you, dear husband, you have just told me who told you about David! Amelia to Beryl to Douglas... simple.

"Oh, Douglas, that's not true at all! I love the light stuff too, but sometimes I need something to get my brain working," she said, smiling. "Are you talking about Beryl?" she asked, feigning innocence. "I didn't think she was good enough to perform professionally. That's surprising. But how nice that you kept up with her after she left Washington. It would be fun to see her again." Douglas, of course, would make sure that would never happen.

"Er, yes." said Douglas, folding up like a salted snail. Not going to pick that one up, eh, thought Thalia, but then she wondered whether she had been unkind. Perhaps she was sometimes too sharp, maybe Douglas responded to her by withdrawing emotionally. Could that be what Pam is seeing?

"Where do you plan to go first, Pam?" she inquired. "There's a lot to explore here in Brussels also, but you can do that in between visiting other places. I'm planning a trip to London as soon as I can leave Minerva here with Douglas and the nurse."

"What?" exploded Douglas, "this is the first I've heard of this." Suddenly remembering Pam's presence, he calmed down. "Let's talk about it later."

But Thalia didn't want to let it go. "Oh, I'm sure Pam doesn't mind. I was just thinking of visiting Dorrie and John, and I suppose I could take the kids with me in that case. Dorrie has become a jolly tyrant with kids, the more there are to organize the better! And there are nursemaids and housekeepers galore! Our two could stay with her, and Pam and I could have a couple of days in London together--I'm longing to go back!"

Pam, who had been quietly observing the tension between Thalia and Douglas, said, "I am really considering heading for Paris first. It's late enough in the year that there are probably fewer tourists now, and I'll be able to visit the places I've looked forward to seeing. Tally, could you come with me?"

Immediately Thalia saw the delicious possibilities of visiting Paris! A super Douglas tail-twister! Forget being kinder to him! If she and Pam were in Paris, she would be staying with Douglas in his hotel room, and he would be obliged to entertain them part of the time. How would he be able to see Clemence? "That's a fabulous idea, Pam! Let's do it! What do you think, Douglas?"

"Ummm, well... perhaps. We need to think about it. Hard for you to leave the baby while you're nursing her."

"She will have to be trained to take a bottle too from time to time, so for a short time it would be fine. Not right away, but in a few weeks."

So thoughtful of Minerva's comfort now, the baby you didn't want, thought Thalia. Now that she's here, real, a living, breathing child, do you ever think of that? You wished the black Pool of the Drowned Children for her. Don't you remember?

Chapter Twenty-two

Nigel and Thalia

Pam went to Paris without Thalia, who had decided that teasing Douglas was a poor idea for the moment. If their estrangement was so evident that Pam, an outsider, could see it, Thalia knew that something needed to change if she wanted the marriage to continue. But did she want that--remain in the marriage as Douglas's wife in every way? She wanted to remain in Europe, she did not want to return to either Australia or the United States. It appeared at present that the only way to do that was to stay with Douglas, until she could establish her own credentials for European residence, if that were possible.

It was quiet in the little garden of their house, a pleasant place for reflection, with a few birds twittering quietly in the trees, and late autumn colors still glowing in the long light of the afternoon sun. I wonder who planted this garden, Thalia thought, chose the shrubs and vines so carefully, and tended it to bring it to its mature beauty. The clematis vine is subtly perfect with its silvery seed pods against the old brick wall, next to the espaliered pear trees so typical of European gardens, where nature seems to have been subdued and bent to the uses of domesticity. The trees are flattened to grow against the wall to save space, and the tiny pears grow so tidily, so easy to reach for picking, they seem eager to wait in an old basket on the kitchen bench for the cook to use them for preserves, perhaps, or a pear tart to be served with thick yellow cream. Australian gardens are different from these--half-wild, semi-tamed, the cough-drop scent of the bush over them and the rainbow parrots flashing screeching through the eucalyptus trees like noisy lightning, and the little blue lizards sunning themselves on the pathways. Why am I thinking of Australia now, she asked herself, if I don't want to go there again. And if I don't want to go there, why do I still think of it as "home"? Perhaps it's because life there for me was so much simpler, clearer--I was young, maybe too young for the decisions I made--thank heavens I never had to consider abortion as a choice to be made.

It's not that I think abortion is always wrong, she thought. There are times, I suppose, when there are good reasons for it, but it should never be used for someone's convenience. That's wrong, just wrong, and I can't accept that Douglas would try to make me do that because he didn't want another child.

From her point of view, she needed to stay married to Douglas but, since his demand that she abort the child that was Minerva, she had not resumed intimacy with him. He had tried to convince her that his masculinity was at stake, that without regular intimacy he was unable to function normally, and that she was endangering his ability to do his job. So far, Thalia was unmoved. Her anger made her impervious to his pleading and bluster. She'd heard this teenage argument from boyfriends before, anyway, and it was no more successful now than then. And presumably, his masculinity was now protected by his relations with Clemence.

If I need to stay married to Douglas, what are my assets to achieve that, she wondered. First, I suppose, the children. I believe that he cares about them--both of them, now that Minerva is a reality. Would he want to stay married rather than hurt them by divorcing me?

Second, his career. A presentable wife is a major asset, almost a necessity, to fulfill the social obligations which come from higher rank in European bureaucracy. Does Douglas understand this? A question for me here also, though. Will it become easier in the future for women to achieve high rank themselves, and therefore change this situation and devalue my position?

And, third, the manuscript, of course. Will its value diminish with time? So far, the book appears to have become a modern classic, and an allegation of plagiarism would be sensational and affect its value to Douglas.

Before I go any further with these considerations, I need to talk to Nigel. There are questions, ideas, concerns swirling in my mind that need to be laid out and discussed with him. It's time to take Danny and Minerva and visit Dorrie in England. I've been constantly occupied during the months since Danny and I arrived in Brussels--locating a place to live, settling him in nursery school, moving into the house, and then Minerva's birth. Now it seems like time for a change and a rest. Not forgetting either the discovery of Douglas's infidelity with Clemence Laulan. His boss's wife! I'll take the big car--he isn't using it while he's in Paris--and drive to England with the children and Cecile, and if we bump into Nigel, it will be a happy accident.

Dorrie was delighted at the prospect of seeing them in England, welcoming the children and Cecile, but nixing the idea of Thalia driving Douglas's car. "You are not going to drive a left-hand drive car on the left side of the road in heavy traffic from Dover to London! That would be crazy! I know you have driven on the left in Australia, but it's different when the steering wheel is on the wrong side. I won't let you kill yourself and the kids! Drive to Ostend and leave the car at one of the hotels, and I'll bring the family circus and get you at the ferry in Dover. John is going to be in New Zealand for two months, so I will be by myself with all these kids and animals." She stopped to draw breath, then continued, "I think I will come to London with you and leave the chaos here. I'm pregnant again, so a London shopping trip would be perfect. New clothes for Number Four! For me, not the baby."

A phone call to Douglas in Paris confirmed his agreement with Dorrie. "Good idea, Thalia. Take a little trip. I'm not going to be back for a while. Have some fun. Do you need money?" Things must be going well with Clemence, thought Thalia, if he's willing to part with his money. Book must still be selling too.

"Well, I would like to stay at the Connaught again, so a little extra would be helpful," she said, planning hastily, "and I don't think Dorrie wants to share a room." And neither do I, for that matter. I need my own room.

All was accomplished, and Thalia, Daniel, Minerva, and Cecile set off for their trip to England. The drive to Ostend was smooth, but the crossing of *La Manche, (*the Channel)was rough. Cecile, on her first time out of continental Europe, was seasick. "Oh," she wailed "I feel 'orrible! I want my *maman*!" When Thalia tried to comfort her, she replied, "*Oolala*! When a French girl *est... malade...* , she wants first her *maman*, and second her *eau de Vichy*!" Since neither was available on board, Thalia left her to her travail while she and Daniel enjoyed watching the waves and spray from inside the glassed-in cabin, and Minerva slept the sleep of the well-nourished baby.

Dorrie's big car waited at the passenger exit from the terminal, with the boys waving and shouting a welcome to Danny, the dogs barking, and Dorrie giving orders, "Redfield, I told you not to bring Boris! Boris, shut up! Martin, give your sister her dummy and sit with her, please," while Lorna, Dorrie's baby girl, began to cry, Boris the borzoi whined and scratched with the excitement of greeting new people, and Thalia attempted to organize her group, get the luggage into the boot, and pay the porter.

"Cecile, we're on firm ground now. Can you please take Minerva while I get us into the car? Just take her and go sit in the back seat, and stop crying, for heaven's sake. You can help Martin with Lorna too." At last, the confusion subsided, Boris calmed down, and all but Thalia were settled in the car, where there appeared to be no room for her.

"See you at home, Thalia," shouted Dorrie, as she slowly pulled the big car away. Laughing, she added, "Nigel's right behind. I thought you'd like to ride with him this time."

There wasn't time for Thalia to protest, even had she wanted to. There was Nigel, driving his ridiculously small car, leaning over to open the door for her and saying, "Hop in quick, love, there's a big lorry treading on my tail!"

Love, she thought. The word “love”, the colloquial British “love”, used for anyone from nine to ninety? Or something deeper, perhaps hard for me to recognize for sure and certain?

Chapter Twenty-three

Agreement

"Nigel! Lovely to see you, but... how did you know we were coming?"

"Wouldn't you like to know?" he replied. "I have my secrets, but when I get to know you better, perhaps I'll share."

Thalia decided to ignore this and continued, "Oh, Dorrie told you, of course. I don't know what happened to sweet, softspoken Dorrie! No ladylike manners any more. She was so funny back there, shouting 'Shut up, Boris!' She seemed a little prissy on board *Oriana*, but not now."

"You should hear her swear--must have studied with the stable boys!" Nigel replied. "I think it's just that she's grown up and become a mother, and anyway people like the Magnus clan can get away with a lot more than us ordinary common folk. "Sir" or "Lady" in front of your name gets you a lot of latitude in this country.

"Does Dorrie have a title?"

"No, but her father does. He was MP for his district, got a baronetcy from the Queen for something, so now he's Sir

Dorian Magnus, retired, very grand and a bit pompous. But never mind that right now. We need to talk. How much time do we have before *you* have to be a mother again?"

"About four hours, I think, before I need to be back to take care of Minerva. And yes, I agree that we need to talk."

Thalia picked up a lock of her hair and began to twist it in her fingers. Nigel, too distracted to drive in the heavy motorway traffic, turned down a side street and stopped.

"Thalia, my redhaired Irish warrior queen, I love your hair, but why are you twisting it like that? Are you nervous? If it's because of me, you mustn't be. I've been in love with you since you showed up talking about the albatross that night. I tried to forget about you when you married Douglas, but I couldn't." He reached over and caught the hand that was pulling at the hair, imprisoning it in a gentle grip but when she pulled it free, he let it fall and stroked her cheek softly instead. This time she didn't pull away, but turned toward him, putting her hand on his arm and saying, "Oh, Nigel, it's so good to see you! Is there somewhere we could talk around here?"

"I think there's a village up the road a bit. There's probably a tea room where we can talk and give the local ladies some excitement. '*Did you see those two holding hands in the corner? And she was wearing* ***trousers****!*

Depraved, I call it. They drank coffee in the ***afternoon****! They must be Americans.'"*

"I hope there's a pub--I know ladies' tea rooms," she replied. "They're the same in Australia. Frilly curtains, flowered china, cucumber sandwiches with the crusts cut off, and vicious gossip a prominent item on the menu. But, do you mind my wearing trousers?"

"Well, I would like a miniskirt better, but you look good. What happened to the mini?" He chuckled a little, then said, "Too bad you didn't ask men for their opinions."

There was a village pub, and they found seats by the fire in the snug. "Nigel, tell me more about yourself and your family. What you said about Dorrie's family, the Magnuses, made me realize I know almost nothing about you, except that you're an actor. Where did you go to school?" She stopped and laughed at herself for a moment "Listen to me--that's an Australian cliché! In Sydney, they ask 'How much money do you have?', in Melbourne they ask 'Where did you go to school?', but in Perth they say "Welcome, mate. Have a beer!"

"Is that a hint? Would you like a beer?"

She laughed, "Oh, not a hint! The beer would be warm, anyway – ugh. But a sherry would be nice."

When he came back from the bar with her sherry and his pint of lager, he sat down and said, "Thalia, I asked you once to run away with me. I meant it, but I understand now that you couldn't. Things have changed a lot for both of us though, and I think it's time we reconsidered matters between us. My career's going well, I am well-paid, making money and able to support you..."

She cut him off. "Nigel, I know. As you say, things have changed for both of us." She stopped, trying to assess the situation and keep control of it. To her, this seemed like a negotiation; in the past she felt she had lost control when negotiating with David Springer and this time she hoped to manage the discussion in order to achieve what she herself wanted. But of course, Nigel isn't David, is he? Have there been other women in his life all these years since *Oriana*? He's very attractive, so I suppose there must have been. But it looks as if there isn't anyone at present, if his interest in me is genuine. Should I tell him what I have in mind? Perhaps honesty would be best.

"Has there been anyone in your life since *Oriana*?" she asked, surprising herself with the candor.

"If you mean have I slept with anyone, I think you must know the answer to that. Of course I have. I promised to love you, but not to be celibate forever.

Thalia turned this thought over in her mind for a while, then, "Were any of them important? Are they still in your life?"

"None important, but some are still in my life--I work with them occasionally, but we've all gone past those encounters. They were fun but not important and none of them made any difference to the way I feel about you. I'm not on stage tonight, but I have to be back tomorrow. Must you go to Dorrie's tonight? Maybe we could find a little inn somewhere around here to spend the night."

"No, I need to be there for Minerva. I can certainly leave her with Dorrie's nurse and Cecile, but not without planning. And anyway, I haven't decided anything yet." A lie, she thought. I have decided to be unfaithful to Douglas with Nigel, but I want to decide the when, the how, and the setting. No to a tiny room under the eaves, smelling of cigarette smoke and mildew, and a double bed with a slumping mattress and not enough covers. And a leering landlady. "I have a reservation at the Connaught for a couple of days, starting Wednesday. Are you available to spend some time with me?"

Nigel's reaction surprised her. Far from the joyous shout she expected, he responded cautiously. "Are you inviting me to stay with you at the Connaught? I don't want to anticipate making love to you but find that you were just teasing me. You need to do a bit better than that, Thalia, or risk being called unpleasant names."

I am losing control, Thalia thought. "I think so. I'm scared, Nigel. I have been faithful to Douglas all this time, but I can't say he's reciprocated. I'm nervous. Can we move more slowly?"

Rubbing his hand over his head and around the back of his neck, the image of the baffled male, he said grudgingly, "Alright. I'll slow down. I'll meet you in London on Wednesday. And now, let's get to Doone Haven Stables. They'll be wondering where we are."

As he drove them to Dorrie's, she said, "Tell me about your family. I really want to know so that I can understand you better."

"Oh, not much to tell. Theatre people, mostly, so sometimes people like Dorrie are a bit haughty about us, but they are flattered when we come to their parties because we are different and they think we're amusing. And John has democratized Dorrie a whole lot with his antipodean ways! But my family's pretty conventional, really."

"Do they expect you to marry well, to settle down and be a dutiful husband to some English rose?"

“No,” he said, laughing, “they hope that I will stay single, make love to every pretty actress I meet, maybe a bastard or two in the mix to scandalize them and their friends, and generally be a complete London rake. Is that what you want me to say?”

“You’re laughing at me.”

“A little bit. But do you remember when we met in London when you were pregnant with Minerva?”

“Yes, I do remember. You were so diffident, so hesitant, that I thought you must have forgotten our earlier meetings, and that you hated me.”

“You were pregnant with another man’s child. That was very hard for me to take. You laughed, said something about “That’s what happens to young married women”, but I was crushed. I wanted it to be our child that you were carrying, our child that we had created with our love, our child that we would raise together. I was devastated. I couldn’t think about anything else for months. I tried to write to you but I couldn’t find words to tell you how I felt. But here you are, and maybe we have a chance now to change things. I suppose it depends now on you and what you want.

“I don’t care what people think, my family or anyone. I am building a reputation in my chosen career, how I spend my life outside the theatre is my business. I choose you, Thalia. You once said to me that you chose Douglas. How has that worked out for you? Are you ready to make a different choice?"

Chapter Twenty-four

Connaught Hotel & London Again

"Welcome, Mrs. Barton, nice to see you again." said the suave young man behind the reception desk at the Connaught Hotel, his manner as polished as the gleaming surfaces of the desk and floor of the foyer. "We've given you a different room this time when she made the reservations, Mrs. Ridd thought you would like one of the small suites, where you would have a bit more room."

Thalia and Dorrie had come up to London that morning, Dorrie driving the small car. The car had been whisked away by one of the doormen as soon as their luggage was out, and would presumably reappear when needed again. Taxis though seemed to be more useful in London, where traffic and lack of parking made the use of a car impractical. The tube, Thalia thought, would suit her very well, but it appeared that Dorrie didn't plan on using that method of getting around and had tried to discourage her. "It's dirty, Thalia, and noisy, and so crowded! I don't take it any more."

"Is it safe?" asked Thalia, remembering stories about the New York subways.

"Oh, I suppose so, if you don't mind the people, but you don't need to use it. Just take a taxi, or walk. London's lovely for walking--so many things to see. We can take a walk later, if you would like."

"Perhaps," said Thalia, thinking that she would prefer to wait at the hotel until Nigel showed up. Dorrie left, saying she would show herself to her room, and issuing imperious orders about her luggage, requests for tea and scones delivered to her room, and instructions about which phone calls should be directed to her room, which should have messages taken, and which should be ignored. Thalia thought she could see some sly smiles among the desk staff. Perhaps they were familiar with Dorrie and her demands?

"Thalia, shall I ring you later? What about dinner?"

"I don't know. I'll let you know." As she followed the well-tailored young man up the grand staircase, she wondered how long it would be until Nigel arrived. Her escort opened the door to her suite and held it for her to enter. Sunlight filled the room, laying bright patches on the blue and white Chinese carpet on the floor and the soft blue sofas which stood in the center of the room. The ambiance of the room was tranquil and soothing, contrasting with the ebullient energy of the London streets. The staff person indicated her overnight bag resting on the luggage rack in the adjoining bedroom, and made a courteous exit.

Thalia explored the luxurious rooms, noting the expensive linens on the large soft bed, the thick towels and the Floris soaps and perfumes, marked "By Appointment to the Queen", in the bathroom. Curtained in filmy white fabric, the bedroom was shadowy, aqueous, its light mysterious and romantic.

She moved her overnight bag to the bed to open it, revealing the lingerie purchased at Maison Gregoire on the day she had learned for sure of Douglas's infidelity. Is it the time to bring it out now? To bring to life the little fable she and the young *vendeuse* had concocted that day?

An extravagant revenge purchase, she realized, intended to soothe her battered pride, to hurt the one who had caused her pain. But I already knew he was unfaithful, she thought. Why did I react so strongly to that news? Was it that my marriage had become fuel for the gossip mill of Brussels' expatriates? My pregnancy, resented by Douglas? Or that I had expected praise for the achievement of moving the family here, winding up our lives in Alexandria and starting to settle here? But there had been no praise, no admiration, just Douglas's constant demands for more effort. And then the public humiliation of hearing my failure as a wife mocked and derided by the women I had hoped would be my friends. I suppose it was all of it, plus the hormones and stresses of pregnancy, that caused such an emotional storm.

And then there was the revelation that Douglas knew about David Springer and our affair on board *Oriana*. Douglas and I haven't had that out yet, but we definitely need to discuss it. But somehow that he learned about it from Beryl, one of his little *amours*, makes a difference, at least to me. He learned about my infidelity (although technically, we weren't married at the time) from the person he was sleeping with while he was married to me, and that makes a huge difference.

A soft knock at the door interrupted her calculations. She hurried to the door, expecting to see Nigel there, but instead she found a young waiter with a tea cart--translucent china teacups and saucers, a teapot with a pretty cozy pretending to keep the contents hot, and a silver cake stand offering scones, tiny slices of seed cake, smoked salmon sandwiches, and *petit fours*. Alongside this traditional British tea were two champagne flutes and a bottle of Veuve Clicquot champagne.

Thalia, for whom tea was a daily ritual and pleasure, was pleased but surprised. "I didn't order this. It's lovely, but it must be meant for some other room" she said, but the waiter was adamant. "No, madam, it is for your room." Wheeling the trolley into the sitting room, he positioned it carefully in front of two chairs grouped by the window, and left with a courteous "Thank you, madam."

It must be from Nigel, she thought. How sweet and thoughtful of him. The champagne reminded her of the romp on board *Oriana* with David Springer, her first sexual adventure. She smiled, remembering the fun of that, although also feeling a little regretful. It had been indiscreet she knew now, and probably unwise as well, and the prospect of a showdown with Douglas over it was daunting. Still, he was hardly in a position to complain too much, with Clemence, Beryl, and probably others on his souvenir dance program.

Another soft knocking at the door sent her running to the door to open it to Nigel and afternoon delight. Eagerly flinging it open, she said "How lovely to send me champagne..." only to stop in consternation. Douglas stood there, smiling widely and saying "Surprise, darling! Time for a second honeymoon! Aren't you going to ask me in?"

"Douglas! What are you doing here?"

"What kind of a welcome is that, dear wife? Aren't you pleased to see me?"

"Ummm... yes, of course, but I'm just a bit surprised. I thought you were in Paris with... um... some kind of conference."

"I should be, but when I realized that you would be in London without the children for a couple of days, I decided to join you and spend some time repairing our marriage. We've grown apart the last year or so, and I miss you. So, here I am, and we can see London together. And also spend some time in this lovely suite." Peering past her toward the bedroom, "That bed looks very comfortable. Shall we try it out now?"

Thalia, attempting to collect her thoughts, was barely able to speak. "I must call Dorrie. We had planned to go for a walk and have dinner together. Let me call her and tell her the news."

Finding a telephone in the little entrance hall, she asked the operator to connect her with Mrs. Ridd's room, and when she had Dorrie on the line, said "Dorrie, Douglas just arrived, so I can't have dinner with you tonight."

Dorrie responded "What! Douglas is here! Oh, how awful! Can he hear you now?"

"I suppose so."

"What do you want me to do? Shall I ring Nigel for you?"

"Oh, yes, what a good idea! That would be very nice."

"Alright. How long is Douglas staying?"

Thalia forced a little laugh. "He says it's a second honeymoon. Imagine my surprise!"

"Oh, dear. Ring me if there is anything more I can do. Maybe lunch tomorrow?"

"Let me see. I'll ring you in the morning. Bye for now."

She disconnected the call and walked back to the bedroom, where she found Douglas pulling her things out of the suitcase. "I suppose these are what I paid that fancy pants Frenchman for, hmm? I recall being startled by the bill." Pawing through the lingerie, he pulled out a nightgown, an ethereal silvery green, and threw it to Thalia. "Put this on for me." he ordered. "And let your hair down too. I like this color with your hair."

She took the garment and started to the bathroom in order to change into it, but Douglas stopped her. "No. You can change right here. I want to watch you. Come on, Thalia. You can't be shy with me, and it's been a long time since we made love. Get with it."

She did as he asked, and with Thalia wearing the gown intended to delight another man, they made love in their old familiar way, their bodies so accustomed to one another that, even though she had been reluctant, she enjoyed it and felt fulfilled and comforted. Guilt and Nigel would wait for tomorrow.

Chapter Twenty-five

Confrontation

The morning light, gray and shadowless, filtered softly through the curtained window, implying a typical London drizzle outside. The traffic sounds were muted by the hotel's triple glazing and soundproofing, but still Thalia could recognize that she was waking somewhere other than her bedroom in the house in Brussels. With consciousness came the memory of last night, and the current view of Douglas's sleeping form next to her in the bed. Remembering their lovemaking of last night, she couldn't believe that she had consented without a fuss. Horrified, she sat up suddenly, and pulled on her robe to hide her nakedness as she put her feet on the floor. Douglas, disturbed by her movements, woke up and reached out to pull her into bed again, but she evaded him.

"Come back here," he said in a throaty morning voice, "and let's talk about things. We've needed that for a long time, Tally, and I hope we can patch things up between us. I've missed you."

Thalia, choosing not to answer this, instead said, "I'm going to get dressed, then I'll order breakfast. Do you want something to eat?" as she pulled together some clothes and headed for the bathroom. "If you're hungry, there's all the stuff that you ordered in the other room. Go and eat that."

"What stuff?" asked Douglas, heaving himself out of bed. Thalia, seeing his naked form, retreated hastily to the bathroom, closed the door, and began to dress. She heard him moving around, swearing as he blundered into something, then he shouted, "So, Thalia? Champagne on the tea cart? Two glasses? Just what is going on?" Oh, the cart, Thalia remembered. There was champagne on the cart as well as tea. I thought Nigel sent it, then when Douglas showed up, I decided it was his work. What do I say? Is there any way to rescue this situation?

"Dorrie and I were planning a little celebration--you know, girls get-together, shopping trip, off-the-domestic leash, that's all."

"Hmmph. French champagne. Nothing too good for you girls! And all the fancy frillies from Frenchie Greg--was that for Dorrie too? Are you cheating on me, dearest?"

Thalia took a deep breath while she decided her course, then, through the door, "Not yet, but I am planning on it. And why not? You've been unfaithful to me now for years... still are, with your boss's wife, for heaven's sake! Smart way to play the career game!"

"Who's the lucky guy, huh? Some bloke from jolly old Down Under? Or no--wait! The one on the ship? That must be it. You were cheating even before we got married!" No pretense of playfulness in his voice now, he said, "I won't give you a divorce, you know."

Coming out of the bathroom and confronting him, she said, "What do you want, Douglas? To punish me for my idiotic mistake on the ship? I was stupid, I freely admit it. I was too young, lacking common sense, shouldn't have been out on my own. And I'm sorry, if that helps." She stopped, reading his face and seeing no softening there after her apology.

"What do *you* want, Thalia? You got what you wanted when I brought you out of Australia, out of that smug suburban life you had there. Remember that? You told me I opened the world for you! You were giddy with the freedom, silly and affected as you learned about the world, making a fool of yourself with your pretensions. But no divorce for you, if that's your plan. You can just stay by my side and act like you are a real wife."

"Oh, I don't think I will do that. I will stay with you so that you are acceptable as a senior bureaucrat in Brussels to protect your income for the sake of the children, but not as what you call 'a real wife'. You will *never again* order me to sleep with you as you did last night."

"Well, you didn't seem all that reluctant. And just how do you think you can make that happen?"

"By releasing the manuscript of A Family's Pain with your brother's name on it if you should try to force me into your bed."

"Nobody's going to believe you. Your story would be meaningless."

"I told you before that I have a copy of the manuscript. With your brother's name written on it--Peter Barton. And the date he finished it."

Silence. Douglas stared at her, then turned away, gathered his clothes from the floor and went into the bathroom. A short time later, somewhat untidily groomed, he emerged and made his way to the outer door where he stopped, glowered at her, and said, "We will talk again, Thalia," then left the room, slamming the door behind him.

She sat down hard on one of the blue sofas, trying to calm herself. Time for planning is over now and battle is joined. First, I'll call Dorrie and then Nigel. But before she could reach the phone, it rang. Dorrie was on the other end of the line, calling from her room in the hotel.

"Can you talk?" she asked hastily.

“Oh, yes, thank heavens! He’s gone.”

“Nigel?”

“No! Douglas! He stayed all night.”

“Oh, my goodness! What did you do?”

“What do you mean?”

“Oh!” Flustered, Dorrie tried to recover. “You know what I mean!”

“Yes, I suppose so. We went to bed together. I can’t believe I did that. It just seemed easier than resisting him, but now I am so confused.”

“Oh, you poor dear. Would talking about it with me later be helpful?”

Thalia went on without answering her. “Then this morning we talked, there was a confrontation and the topic of David Springer came up, I mentioned Clemence, and I told him about the manuscript. He slammed out the door, saying ominously ‘we’ll talk, Thalia’. It was a threat, I think.”

“What are you going to do now?”

Thalia shrugged, then realizing that Dorrie couldn't see her, said, "I don't know. Wait and see what happens next, I suppose."

There was a soft knock at the door, and she hung up hastily after promising to call Dorrie later. Approaching the door cautiously, hoping it wasn't Douglas returning, she opened it, to see Nigel there, his eyes full of pain and concern.

"Are you alright, Tally?" he asked quietly, using for the first time her childhood pet name as he entered the room. Feeling cherished, caressed by his gentle kindness and the loving name, she nodded, then reacting to the tension and stress of the night, began to sob, her body shaking with the violent emotion. Nigel put his arm around her and drew her over to one of the sofas, where he settled her and sat close to her, stroking her hair and trying to soothe her with his voice.

"Tally, let it out now. What happened to upset you so much?"

"I can't tell you. I'm so ashamed."

"Dorrie rang me and told me that Douglas had shown up here unexpectedly, so I didn't come as I had planned. I was worried about you though. Do you want to tell me about it?"

"Not really," she hesitated, "but I will. He accused me of being unfaithful to him, and I said that I hadn't been but that I plan to be, and he said that he won't give me a divorce no matter what, and I said that's fine but I won't be what he calls a 'real wife', and then he found all the pretty lingerie I had bought in Brussels and brought with me to wear when I..."

"When you what, Tally?"

"I guess when I go to bed with you. But you won't want me now, after he made me sleep with him." She started to cry again. "Then I told him I would use the manuscript and expose him, and he left, threatening me with 'We will talk, Thalia'."

"Did he rape you? Is that what you're trying to say?"

"No. It's worse than that. I didn't want to, but I was afraid to refuse so I consented, and I... "she hiccuped, then blew her nose, wiped her eyes, and tried again, "... I sort of enjoyed it! I am a monster!"

Holding both of her hands, Nigel began to laugh, and said, "I'm sorry, but this is farce. Even Oscar Wilde couldn't write it! I don't know about any manuscript, but you can tell me over lunch. Well, looks like we have a decision to make. Tell you what we'll do. Let's check out of here, take your stuff to my place and spend a day in

London, do some shopping, and you can see the show tonight. Then we can decide how we want to proceed from now on. Deal?"

Reassured by his confident decision-making, Thalia began to feel calmer now that it seemed that he wasn't lost to her, and said shakily, "Alright. I don't want to ever see this room again. Let me pack and ring Dorrie."

As they left the hotel, the thin London winter sun shone out from between the clouds for a moment, seeming to bring a promise of spring and the hope of happier things to come. Thalia though had enough happiness for the moment, and for once she felt confident that the future would take care of itself.

Chapter Twenty-six

Thalia's Bangle

Nigel's flat, small, practical and utilitarian, mostly lacked charm although with its long windows looking into a tree-lined square of old brick houses with delicate fan transoms above their brightly-painted doors, Thalia thought that it had good possibilities. "This is Bloomsbury, Thalia," Nigel said. "It's mostly mid-nineteenth-century Victorian, with Georgian here and there. The British Museum is just down there," waving vaguely in the air, "and a lot of writers have lived here. Virginia Woolf, for one. Soho or Covent Garden would be a shorter walk to the theatre for me but it's quieter here."

"Dorrie, do you mind being at the hotel alone?" asked Thalia when she reached her friend on the telephone. "I'm at Nigel's flat, and we have plans for the day. Douglas will probably come looking for me, and I don't want to see him, so I've left the hotel."

Laughingly, Dorrie replied, "Well, I didn't expect to see much of you in London this time anyway, so no worries. What's his flat like?"

Thalia, amused by this typical feminine question, said, "Well, pretty much bachelor stuff. I'll try to get a peek in the bedroom, see if there are any female things in there,…"

"Oh. You haven't been in the bedroom yet?"

"Saucy question, Dorrie. No. Not yet."

"Well, I'll be here until lunchtime tomorrow. Do you want to drive back to Doone Haven with me?"

"Yes, please. I want your advice, and the car's a good place for that. I'll meet you in the lobby."

"What should I tell Douglas if he shows up here again?"

"Oh, I don't know. Tell him you don't know anything. I will have to deal with him eventually, but not now."

Disconnecting, she turned to Nigel who had begun to make breakfast in the kitchen. Wearing an enveloping white apron, he lacked only a toque to appear professional and competent, although the untidy preparations--broken eggshells on the counter, smears of butter, jammy marks on the apron--made her wonder. "Ready in a tick," he said, hastily moving a smoking pan off the gas stove, "tea's made, eggs coming, sit down at the table. Ready in two shakes of a puppydog's tail." He swore under his breath as he poked at the incinerated scrambled eggs in the pan, and said, "I wanted to make you a meal! Hell's teeth, I'm hopeless at it. Why don't we go out?"

She jumped up to help him as he dropped the hot pan, and said, "I'll do it. I don't mind. Let me wear that wonderful apron. Do you have any more eggs? Pour me a cup of tea —milk, no sugar, please, and get out some plates. Got any marmalade?" Of course, being an Englishman he had marmalade, the best and most expensive kind from Fortnum and Mason, and she quickly produced eggs and toast with marmalade. Wrapped in the apron and the warmth of his company, she felt peace like a soft fluffy blanket enfolding her. "Let's just stay here for the day. I'll clean up the kitchen in a minute."

"No," he said "the daily will be here soon, and she'll do that. And besides, I have an errand, and I need you with me. We can come back to change before the theatre. Hurry up, let's go."

"Let me freshen up a bit first," she said, picking up her bag and heading for the bathroom. Passing through the bedroom--big comfy-looking bed, unmistakably male belongings scattered around, with no sign of feminine occupation (an answer for Dorrie) she heard the front door open, and a female British voice called out teasingly from the entrance hall, "Nige, you here? Come out, come out, wherever you are!" Well, thought Thalia, here's a pretty mess! A girlfriend?

She heard the door from the hall to the sitting room open, and Nigel's voice quietly saying something to the newcomer who replied loudly, "Well, you should have warned me! I could have come tomorrow." Again, Nigel said something inaudible, and what Thalia now thought of as The Voice said, "I won't make you late, don't worry, but I need to spend a penny first. Use your loo, please?" as the bedroom door opened and The Voice, a pretty woman with dark curly hair and brown eyes like Nigel's, walked in.

"Hello," she said "I'm Bella, Nigel's big sister. I saw the two plates on the table, and I thought you must have cooked the eggs. Nigel barely knows what those oval white things are unless they're presented to him cooked on a plate. I gave him the apron, to encourage him and try to keep him clean. Who are you?"

"How do you do? I'm Thalia. And yes, I cooked the eggs." Thalia thought she was well-named. Her voice was clear and carrying, rather like a bell, and she was also *Bella,* beautiful--fine-boned, graceful, with deep-set heavily-lashed eyes that reminded her of Nigel.

"I see by the bed that you didn't spend the night here."

Nigel, hovering in the doorway, began to protest, "Bella! Stop…" but both women ignored him.

Thalia, stung by the comment about the bed, retorted, "Would you judge me if I did spend the night here?"

"Depends. What do you want from him?" Bella's tone was imperative, the voice of the English upper-class woman accustomed to controlling dogs, horses and children.

"Well, I'm not completely sure yet, but I suppose I want a long-term relationship with bed but no board. I have my own money."

Then, Thalia wondered why she had answered Bella that way. Why did I tell her that I wanted a long-term relationship with her brother--almost the first thing I said to her? Was it easier for me to do that instead of telling Nigel himself? And what money do I have? Well, it's done. Now Nigel and I must see how to arrange things.

Nigel and Bella spoke simultaneously, but Thalia heard only Nigel. "Thalia, is that what you want? That's what I was hoping for--not the board part but the long -term part." He rushed to her, hugged her tightly and almost knocked her off her feet onto the bed.

"You might wait till I'm gone, little brother," said Bella. "Well, Thalia, you don't appear to be a fortune hunter, and heaven knows, Nige wouldn't be much use if you were, so I'll wander off and let you get on with things. Be kind to him. Now, I'll spend my penny and be gone."

As good as her word, she left. Nigel said, "She is ringing everyone already from the first phone booth she can find, telling the family. My mother will be on the phone any minute, let's get out of here!"

The phone began to ring. "Mother? If I answer, we won't get away for an hour!" said Nigel, and laughing delightedly, they ran out into the quaint street and the cool air without answering it. Nigel tucked her arm through his and pulled her close as they began to walk.

"We're going to take a walk. I want to go to a shop near Bond Street. Can you walk in those shoes?" looking doubtfully at her feet in their pale grey Italian leather shoes. "And you're wearing trousers."

"Does that matter?"

"Well, there are some dining places that won't allow women wearing trousers to enter."

"No! Go on! Why not?"

"I don't know." He paused for a moment, thinking, then "Well, I suppose it's because things are changing so much now, so fast, and some people are having trouble catching up." They stopped at a busy street, Nigel holding Thalia's arm as a big, red, London Transit, double-decker omnibus growled by followed by its cloud of exhaust, a couple of taxis, a black Daimler, and a majestic Silver Cloud Rolls Royce (who's inside, wondered Thalia?).

On the other side of the street, he continued. "It's almost thirty years since the war, and there are still bomb sites around London from the Blitz. The East End is just now being rebuilt, and in places, the bombweeds are still sprouting. Those weeds began colonizing the ruins after the Blitz, but now enough time has passed to allow youth to mature and their ideas to sprout like the weeds and colonize the future. Look at the theatre-- the new plays and films, and the fashions! Lord help us, the fashions! Up till about 1970, women didn't wear trousers in the city at all--maybe for weekends in the country, but now they're everywhere! The excitement is contagious, like the trousers!"

Thalia said, "I don't know whether to laugh or be sad at that. Do you disapprove of my French trousers?"

He said emphatically, "No! You look fab, and they're part of it all--the changes, I mean. I want to be a leader in it! I told you once that I wanted to be a different kind of actor, in a new kind of theatre." He stopped walking, turning her to face him directly. "It's happening, and I hope you will be with me as part of it all. I love you, Thalia. I think I have loved you forever."

Expressionless, she looked at him for a moment, then saying nothing she dropped her gaze, and turned away. Still silent, she began walking, uncertain what to say but knowing that it was time at last to tell Nigel her plan. Would he agree? And would she be able to both keep control of Douglas and their marriage and simultaneously enjoy a life of delightful dalliance with Nigel? But did she love him, she wondered, with the same uncertainty that she had when she had thought about Douglas, when she was leaving Australia. Perhaps I am incapable of loving anyone, she thought sadly.

"Nigel, I've been thinking..." He pantomimed shock and astonishment, then laughed and let her continue, "and would you want to spend a month with me in the summer every year?" She kept walking steadily as if she had a destination in mind, Nigel just keeping pace as he tried to understand what she needed from him.

"So little? I want to be with you all the time, Thalia."

"Well, later perhaps. And there will certainly be opportunities for weekends together, from time to time, if you can get away. But for now I have to stay in the marriage with Douglas for financial stability for me and the kids. He says he won't divorce me. Can you understand?"

"No. You want a *ménage à trois,* and I don't want that. But if you say you must stay with Douglas, then I will respect that, because I respect you and your judgment, but I would rather not. Do you love me?"

"I... I believe I do."

"Then let's give it a go. But I have some conditions too, and we can discuss them later. And, voila! We have reached our destination..." gesturing at the small shop outside which he had stopped. The heavy glass door groaned a little as he opened it, pushing hard with his shoulders in order to move it. "Been here for a hundred years, this door" he said "and never a drop of oil on the hinges!"

"Ahhh, Mr. Somerville," said the elderly proprietor genially, "Haven't seen you for a while. How are your parents? They're well, I hope? And Lady Bella?" (*Lady* Bella, noticed Thalia. What's that about?)

"They're all well, far as I know, Mr. Entwhistle. Has my order come in yet?"

"Yes. It's in the back. Here, Joey--fetch that box for Mr Nigel. And be quick about it, no stopping to talk to the girls back there. Joey's my apprentice, Mr. Nigel. Things aren't what they used to be, not by 'alf they aren't, but he does alright if I keep after 'im."

Thalia and Nigel waited in the shop, Nigel fidgeting uneasily, and Thalia wondering why they were waiting. At last Joey emerged, holding in his hand a small square box covered in green velvet, the green of deep ocean water. Nigel snatched it from his hand and, pulling Thalia into the farthest corner of the shop, said, "Open it, please!"

Wondering, she opened the little box, to find a bangle, a heavy twisted rope of gold centered with a stone, a diamond, clear as shallow water over white sand. "The stone's from my grandmother's engagement ring. I inherited it from her. Will you accept it as my promise of love and fidelity?"

Thalia, astonished by this turn of events, said "A few minutes ago you said that you had some conditions. May I know what they are?"

"Just one. That you give me a child. Not immediately, but as soon as you feel you can. Will you do that?"

Thalia closed the box and handed it back to him, saying as she did so, "Keep this for now. Give it to me when our child is born."

Chapter Twenty-seven

An Evening at the Theatre

As they left Mr. Entwhistle's little shop, (*Established 1845. Purveyors of Fine Jewellery*), Nigel said, "We have to choose: go home in a taxi and eat at home, or eat lunch out and go direct to the theatre. Are you tired?"

"No, I'm not tired, but I am hungry. Is there someplace quiet where we can have lunch and talk? Where they won't frown at my slacks?"

"Well, there's an Italian place along here facing the park, and they're pretty broadminded. Or there's a pub nearby too. But if you're going to be a leader of revolution, you can't worry about frowns."

"I'll let you do the revolution-leading for me. A pub lunch sounds good."

They found a table in the corner of the pub's crowded public bar and Nigel ordered for both of them. The patrons paid no attention to them and the cheerful din continued unabated. Thalia wrinkled her nose at his pint of warm porter, but her lemon squash was cool and sweet, the ploughman's lunch of crusty bread with sharp cheese tasty, and no frowns were cast in the direction of her trousers. "So, here's to our double life!" said Nigel, hoisting his glass. "Just how do you propose we do this? And how do we keep it secret from Douglas?"

"I don't think it will be hard. He doesn't pay much attention to me, as long as he has Clemence. Or someone like her, I suppose. But I think he senses that I'm leaving him now, and what happened last night was an attempt to bring me back into line. He likes power. And I gave it to him when I accepted his infidelities, his lies, his bullying. But no more." She stopped, taking a long breath before continuing, "I am going to use the manuscript."

"You're shaking" he said. "Slow down, it's alright, I'm listening, you need to tell me about that--you've mentioned it twice now. So…?"

"His book. The book that has sold so many copies, made him so much money, given him entree to so many people and places--he didn't write it. And I have proof."

"Who did write it? And what proof do you have?"

"His brother Peter was the author. Peter sent me a copy of the manuscript to read, signed it with his name and dated it too. Then he was killed in an accident before he could start trying to get it published."

"How did Douglas get hold of it?"

"Well, I showed it to him before Peter died, so he knew about it, and I suppose he found the original (mine is a carbon copy) among Pete's things after he died, and took advantage of his position as executor of the will and his parents' ignorance of what was there."

"Where is your copy? Is it safe?"

"I have a safe deposit box in the U.S. in my name. Douglas can't get to it."

"Have you made a will?" Nigel's voice was urgent, and Thalia looked confused.

"No, I don't have a will. Should I?"

"Oh, Lord, Thalia! Yes! You need a will and an executor. Right now you're not safe. You said you threatened him with "the manuscript". Presumably you meant that you would reveal his theft of it — if you just happened to die, he would inherit everything of yours, including that. Problem solved, for Douglas."

Thalia, awakened abruptly from her dream of the night to come with Nigel, said "No, he wouldn't do something like that...," then, remembering Douglas's coldblooded theft of his brother's intellectual property and the wealth it had brought to him, said, "How do I make a will? And an executor--could you be my executor?"

"I think that would be a bad idea, Thalia! But it could be a way to get Douglas to divorce you, and maybe sue us both for something. Let's see…," pondering briefly, he said "there's Bella's husband. I suppose he can make a will. Sir Outerbridge Ripley, Queen's Counsel. He could have his clerk do it. Or perhaps John Ridd could do it?"

"John's in New Zealand, not back for a while." Thalia said, then remembering her question in the shop, "Oh, her husband! Is that why she's "Lady Bella"?"

"Yes. And she's good at it! You should see her do the Gracious Ladywife, wearing twinset and pearls just like the Queen. SO uppercrust. Well, if John's away, then it will have to be the grand, the lofty Sir Outerbridge Ripley. I'll ring Bella and tell her the problem. Let's go home. Quick, not a moment to lose. I have to get to the theatre too. There's a small revision in Act 1, needs to be blocked." He paused, grinning, and said "Just like London in the Blitz--the play must go on!"

Arriving back in the flat, shadowy now in the early February darkness, Nigel phoned his sister. "Bella, could you help me with something?"

"Magic word, Nige?"

"Oh, Bella, don't play Mother with me! Please. This is urgent." He quickly explained Thalia's difficulty, and Bella picked up the urgency in his voice.

"Yes, I see. I hope she's worth all this. I will ring Ootie and tell him the problem. If you are going to be near the phone, I will see if he can ring you back right away."

A few minutes later, Sir Outerbridge (called Ootie) rang back. Thalia listened on the bedroom extension as he said, "Yes, I think I can help. If the lady could come to my office tomorrow, my clerk can set it all up, she can sign, and Bob's yer uncle. So, Nigel. Someone's got her hooks into you at last! Bella says she's a looker!"

Thalia, hearing this, gave a little giggle and Ootie, embarrassed, reverted to Sir Outerbridge's barrister-formality, and he and Nigel rang off. "Come on, you redheaded looker, get moving! I'll get you a seat in the stalls. I'll send my dresser out at the interval to bring you back to my dressing room."

"Should I wear something formal?" she asked, realizing that she wasn't familiar with London theatre customs.

"Umm...medium, not too much. We'll go to The Ivy for dinner after, but it's not a special night--well it is for us, but not for everyone else. Come here... "He put his arms around her, holding her tightly against him and kissed her, at first gently, tentatively, as if he weren't sure of himself, but then more passionately as she responded to him. They began to move together toward the bedroom.

The telephone rang. Nigel swore. "If that's my mother…!"

Thalia laughed ruefully. "She certainly has great timing! Never mind, we don't have time now anyway. We need to go, don't we, for you to be on time?

"Yes," he picked up the ringing phone, saying "Hello, Mother", still pressing Thalia's body against his insistently, juggling the phone with one hand, Thalia with the other. "Mother, I don't have time right now. I am late for work. May I call you tomorrow?" Stopping, he listened for a few moments, then said, "I don't see how Bella could know that, and moreover, why is she saying it? It's no business of hers. Look, I'll call you tomorrow. Love you. Bye."

"What was Bella saying? Was she critical?" asked Thalia apprehensively.

Nigel brushed her question off, responding, "Nothing, really. Just being the annoying big sister."

He left her in the small foyer of the theatre after picking up her ticket from the box office; she was early, and amused herself by looking at the photographs displayed on the walls, photos that included some of Nigel in his current role, and many of other actors of the past or present. Those of Nigel, taken by a well-known photographer, were darkly illuminated, dramatic, moody, presenting him as a poetic, Heathcliffian figure, hardly recognizable to her. A young woman near her sighed to her companion as she studied them: "He looks so romantic! I would love to meet him!"

To which her male companion replied with a sniff "Likes himself a bit too much, if you ask me. Spoiled. Too much attention." As they moved away, Thalia remembered her first conversation with Nigel, how unassuming he had been, and how he had expressed his admiration for the freedom, the unfettered life of the albatross. Romantic? Yes, although I didn't see it then, I was too immature, too impressed by Douglas's man-of-the-world pose and his frankness in discussions of sex. I had no idea about sex. Perhaps Amelia was right, I needed experience, and had I had some before I met Douglas and agreed to marry him, things might have been different. But then, if I hadn't left Australia on *Oriana*, I would never have met Nigel.

The five-minute bell was signaling the opening curtain, and she quickly sought her seat. Second row, stalls, on the aisle. Feeling cosseted and privileged, she awaited the parting of the deep blue velvet curtain, and the telling of a story. The theatre darkened slowly as the lights were lowered, and the audience chatter subsided. To Thalia, this pause had always seemed mystical, magical, a time to prepare oneself for entry to another world.

As the curtain opened, an usher appeared and quietly asked her to allow two people to pass her and occupy the two adjacent seats. Politely she assented, and the newcomers passed quickly but turned to nod their thanks. The recognition was mutual. Settling comfortably into the next seats were Julian and Charmian! Their amazed exclamations caused a small storm of “Sshhh”, “Down in front!”, and “Save it for later!”. Obediently they sat down, laughing at Nigel’s little deception and dying to talk. Charmian leaned over and hissed in her ear, “Took you long enough to wake up.”

Chapter Twenty-eight
To Tether An Albatross

Nigel was the first actor to appear on stage in the opening scene; Thalia was surprised that he seemed tense, not as comfortable on the stage as she had expected from someone with his performing experience. Charmian leaned over to her and said softly, "Is everything alright with you two? He seems nervous." Thalia nodded in agreement, and said nothing, wondering though how Charmian knew anything about her new relationship with Nigel.

The play, set in London of the present day, focused on the problems of entry into Britain of people from Commonwealth nations, former colonies whose people's racial characteristics and economic expectations were very different from those of the native British. Both sides had problems. The new residents had come naively expecting to be welcomed and nurtured by the mother country only to find anger and resentment surrounding them. "No Blacks or Australians Need Apply" read the signs in some boarding-house windows in London, "Go Back Where You Came From" screamed the graffiti on walls in working class districts, and urban warfare seemed to wait round every corner.

Nigel, playing a conservative politician in the leading role, seemed to relax and feel more comfortable as the act proceeded, but Thalia continued to feel that something was worrying him and was eager to see him during the interval. When the lights went up and the audience began to move toward the foyer and the bar, a young Irishman appeared, identifying himself as Nigel's dresser, and escorted Thalia, Charmian and Julian out a side door into a narrow lane beside the theatre. The lane was crowded, neon lights flashed their messages-- "Girls! Girls!", half-naked young women invited customers into their establishments (don't they get cold, wondered Thalia), "Kinky Dancing" read the signs, and neon cocktail glasses poured their colored drinks continuously into bubbling neon puddles, while couples stood embracing, smoking cigarettes, and sheltering from the soft drizzle under shop awnings while standing in line to enter the clubs. "STAGE DOOR" read the sign above a door a little way ahead, and with the young man forging a way through and hardly time to talk, they made their way there. "Soho gets more interesting every day" remarked Julian, "but same old vices, nothing new or different, just more of the same."

As they entered, a young woman walked swiftly toward them, brushing by and exiting rapidly. It's Beryl, the London sparrow, Thalia realized. She stopped to look back but too late, the door had closed and the woman was gone. What was Beryl doing here? Up a narrow iron stair case they were led by Patrick, then down a dark passage cluttered with equipment till they reached Nigel's dressing room, the door marked with his name and a color photograph of a wandering albatross, silhouetted against a deep blue sky.

"Come," they heard, and squeezed in, Julian and Charmian exclaiming at the size and conditions of the tiny dressing room, "Snug, Nige! No cat swinging in here, I can see." from Julian, while Chairman said, "Mirror's too small, so's the light, but your hair looks nice."

Nigel, wearing a silk robe, looked at Thalia, who had appropriated the only chair in the room, "What do you think, Thalia? Impressed?"

"Ummm... I think it's lovely. Why aren't you wearing your costume?"

The others laughed, and Nigel growled, "Stuff it, you lot," and, turning to her, said "So Patrick can press it during the interval."

"Oh," she said, "silly question! I must seem like a real amateur! But what I really want to know is what Beryl was doing here." She paused and looked at Julian and Charmian, studying their faces. "Do either of you know Beryl? I don't remember her last name, but she was in Washington when we were there, and now she's here and I suppose she and Douglas have resumed their... umm... relationship."

Their faces answered her question affirmatively, but Nigel spoke first. "You must have seen her leaving. She was here with Douglas." Again, expressive faces, Thalia's included, but this time showing astonishment and incredulity.

Thalia was the first to find her tongue. "Douglas was here? Why? What did he want?"

"Well…," said Nigel slowly "he challenged me to a duel, something about pistols in Greenwich Park after the show, but I think he thought better of that when I mentioned my Blue for rifle shooting at Cambridge, so he climbed down a bit, said he'd settle for monetary damages…"

"A duel? Damages? For what?" yelled Thalia, propriety and good manners forgotten for the moment. "He wants to be paid for what? C'mon, Nigel, what the bloody hell does he want money for?"

"Well, he was a little incoherent. I think he and Beryl had spent a while in a bar somewhere, but I got the gist. He says the gossip is ruining his good name."

“Gossip? Gossip? What gossip? And a duel?" shouted Thalia, jumping up and knocking over the chair as she did so. “Has my husband gone mad? I have no idea what he’s talking about, but when Beryl is involved, I suspect Amelia’s skinny fingers are stirring the dirtywork pot. Jesus, Mary and Joseph, what a cockup.”

Julian broke in: “Thalia, we’ve heard some talk lately, nothing specific, some gossip about a new person, someone not from the theatre community, Nigel having a *new friend...*” Julian, pouring his beautiful voice onto the situation like a snake charmer’s flute, gently calmed the upset Thalia into quiet.

But Nigel had more to tell. “Beryl said she only wanted to be helpful--hah! She said she’d heard that this new friend has dark red hair, and comes from America or ‘somewhere over there’, and lives some place where they don’t speak English. At that, Douglas began to yell again and talk about shotguns and ‘the way they do things where I come from,’ and Patrick got alarmed and said he was going to call security, so Douglas stormed out, threatening bloody murder and dismemberment and all kinds of things...” He stopped and turned to Thalia, taking her hands and saying, “I’m sorry. Where do we go from here?”

“I have no idea. Wait till he sobers up, I suppose.”

Charmian broke in. “You two need to know that we have been hearing this about you and Nigel for a while now. Some of it from Beryl just now--yes, we’re acquainted with the little slut--but some from reputable people. Can you deal with it, Thalia? I mean, are you strong enough to stand up to gossip?”

“Well, I’ve heard the talk in Brussels about his affair with Clemence, his boss’s wife. I have enough ammunition to silence Douglas if it comes to that aspect, but I don’t think I can stop the talk about Nigel and me. But where did it start? We’ve only been in public together once or twice.”

“My sister’s probably responsible for about three quarters of it!” exploded Nigel. “She dropped in at my flat this morning and was rude to Thalia. And nosy about my life, passing on lurid speculations to my mother.”

Thalia looked uncertain now. Quietly she asked “How important is your family to you, Nigel? If they disapprove of me, will you be hurt by that? Will the gossip seem more brutal because it involves your family members?”

“No. I’ve been on my own for a long time. I broke away when I went to Cambridge, and they don’t try to tie me down any more. I think they are pleased that my career is going well, even though they wish I had done something more in the family line--law, politics, academia."

In a thoughtful tone, he continued, “My mother’s a bit of a free spirit, though, and I think the acting gene comes from her. She loves theatre and my career, and dines out on the scandalous stories I tell her, and I think she’d understand. So a strong no, I won’t be hurt if they don’t approve.”

“Look,” said Thalia “how much can this hurt us then? Douglas is behaving like a lunatic and I have no idea what he wants. He says he won’t give me a divorce, even though I haven’t asked for one. I won’t argue with that, so how can gossip hurt me except that it’s unpleasant to be the target. The children are too young to be aware of it, anyway, and having a mistress won’t affect Douglas’s job. Seems it’s quite the thing in Europe. He gets a polite presentable wife in the ways that matter to him, and I get love and Nigel, and security for me and the children.”

“What are you going to tell Douglas?” asked Charmian, leaning forward from her perch on a corner of Nigel’s makeup table.

“Nothing,” replied Thalia. “We sit tight, ignore the gossip. Douglas must do the same—since he’s the one responsible for most of it, he needs to behave himself and be more discreet. Cut out Beryl, she’s a gossip fountain, and he doesn’t need her when he has Clemence. Nigel is in London, I’m in Brussels, we meet somewhere faraway in the summer, and I will take on talking to Douglas about all this. He will behave, I guarantee you."

As she paused for breath, they heard three musical chimes sound from the corridor, and a voice on the loudspeaker said "Places please for Act Two. Five minutes to curtain." Nigel hastily took off his robe and began to dress, but Thalia wasn't quite done.

"So," she continued "if it won't hurt Nigel's career and I suspect it won't then I say let's ignore it. In fact, why not make it worthwhile?" Moving solemnly across the narrow room to face Nigel, she said gravely, "Nigel Somerville, will you promise in front of these witnesses to spend at least one month, more if possible, with me every summer from now until forever?"

Julian and Charmian were still and quiet, waiting for what might happen next.

Nigel, with a huge grin, said, "Thalia, I thought you'd never ask! Yes, yes, yes, a million times yes! And now I'm late! I'm first on stage again." Saying, "sorry I can't do better than this, makeup will smear," he pecked lightly at her cheek, then rushed out the door.

In the silence which followed his exit, Julian was the first to speak. "Thalia, why don't you want to marry Nigel?"

She sighed, saying "I was afraid you'd ask that. You see right through me, Julian. Because I don't think Nigel can be tethered. He's the wandering albatross, faithfully following his course, never deviating, never changing, but never tied to one place. Albatrosses mate for life, you know, but then spend most of their lives separated by ocean from their mates, coming together at long intervals for short periods. I don't want to be the ancient mariner, the one who kills the albatross, by binding it with solemn vows and legal tethers and tying it to a static life. I would destroy his and my hopes for happiness."

Chapter Twenty-nine

After the Theatre

At the end of the performance, Nigel sent a message with Patrick that Thalia should come backstage and wait for him so that they could go to the restaurant together, but in view of the gossip surrounding them, she decided to accompany Julian and Charmian and leave Nigel to join them later. She would spend the night at his flat, and return to Doone Haven Stables with Dorrie the next day, after making her will with Ootie's clerk.

The Ivy was crowded when they arrived. As they entered, there was a little hush as the habitués turned toward the door to see if this were someone famous, worthy of applause and admiration as they walked toward their table. Most people were disappointed by seeing only Thalia with Julian and Charmian, but there were a few who whispered, "Is that her? Who is that with her?"

And at least one who knew her, and called her name from behind the coiling smoke of the cigarette she held--Amelia, seated at a table with Beryl. Thalia, surprised by this, stopped walking but Charmian took charge and pushed her toward the table where the waiter stood to usher them into their seats on the green banquette. She called out, "In a moment, Amelia! Let us get settled first!," then, turning to Thalia, whispered, “do you want to talk to them at all?” Thalia shook her head, and Charmian called again to Amelia, “Perhaps later, we’ll stop by your table.” Amelia turned to Beryl, and the two had a brief intense conversation, Amelia shaking her head in disagreement.

Thalia’s group settled at the table, and Julian ordered drinks for them. As the waiter departed, Amelia stood up and began to walk toward them, with Beryl trying to hold her at their table.

As she reached them she said, “I think it’s only fair to warn you that Douglas is on his way here, to have dinner with Beryl and me. He’s feeling pretty argumentative right now and he’s been drinking, so I think a scene is quite likely.” She began to return to her table but stopped and gave her familiar throaty laugh, “So, Thalia, better warn Nigel to stay away tonight!”

As she resumed her seat at the table with Beryl, the front door opened to admit Nigel, accompanied by his sister Bella and her husband Ootie. “So, where is she, this woman who’s finally caught you, Nigel?” boomed Ootie in the voice of the Queen’s Counsel who thrilled the courtrooms of the Old Bailey in important cases.

Nigel caught sight of Thalia and her group at their table, and guided Ootie and Bella past Amelia and Beryl, who were silent as they passed. “Right down here, Ootie.

Thalia, may I introduce my brother-in-law, Sir Outerbridge Ripley."

"How do you do? We already met on the phone this morning." said Thalia, "I believe we have an appointment tomorrow in your rooms." Ootie, lofty and legally learned as he was, still liked a pretty face and beamed as he sat down next to her.

"I look forward to it, dear lady! The morning will shine brighter for it!" His elephantine, old-fashioned gallantry amused Thalia, and she was about to reply with a flirtatious remark when there was the sound of a loud dispute at the entrance, and everyone turned to see the *maitre d'hotel* and a couple of waiters attempting to hold back a loud and inebriated Douglas, with Beryl sniggering behind them.

"I know she's here!" shouted Douglas, struggling in the determined grip of the young waiters, and managing to break free and charge down the center aisle of the restaurant, the narrow carpeted path where celebrities and the fashionable paraded their elegance nightly. Douglas, his dishevelment underlining his intoxication, saw Thalia and stopped in front of her, while Nigel and Julian stood up to protect her. He began to shout again, "So you think you can threaten me? Think you can hurt me by lying about me? I'll stop you! I'll make sure you can't do it. Better back off now, you lying bitch." With that, he turned, swatting aside the waiters who were trying to restrain him and walking quickly to the door, he left, with Beryl following him and giving a rude finger sign to Thalia's group as she did so.

"Dear me," said Ootie, "is she a close acquaintance, Thalia?"

Bella said, "Ootie, it's not the time to try to be funny. Please be quiet."

Ootie subsided as Nigel summoned the waiter and said, "Thalia and I are leaving without waiting for dinner. Please be my guests. The waiter will put it on my account. I'm sorry, but I think Thalia needs to leave."

She nodded, and stood up close to Nigel, shaking after the scene with Douglas. "Sorry, everyone. I'll see you all soon. Goodnight."

Outside in the street, quiet now that the theatres were closed for the night, Nigel put his arm around her protectively, saying, "Go ahead and cry, love. I might join you! What a mess." Looking around for a taxi, he said, "Let's go home. It's time."

They sat silent and close in the taxi, holding hands in the darkness. At last she turned her face to him and he leaned over to her, kissing the tears away tenderly as she continued to cry. "We're home. Let's go. Everything's going to be alright, you'll see," coaxing her gently out of the cab and into his flat. "Hungry? You haven't eaten much today," he said, and that made her laugh.

"Yes, I am hungry! I'll make us an omelette. Do you have another pan? This one... "holding up the burned pan from the morning, "is ruined. It will never be the same. You can make the tea." So, reprising their breakfast that morning, they sat down at the kitchen table to enjoy food in one another's company. Then, without fuss or drama, they went to bed together. This time there were no phone calls and no one interrupted them.

Chapter Thirty

The Morning After

"Let's make love one more time," whispered Thalia softly to Nigel in the morning, "it's a long while till summer." Nigel had no objection. And very nice too, she thought. No shooting rockets, no Wagneresque high emotion or drama, nothing but gentleness, loving kindness and consideration, but satisfaction both physical and emotional for both. Thalia found his lovemaking more sophisticated than she had expected; presumably he had spent time with a number of partners during the years since they had met on board *Oriana*. Not sure how to feel about that, she set it aside to think about.

"Where shall we go, for our first summer together?" she asked, as they lay together, warm, drowsy and relaxed. "Do you have any ideas? Any limitations?"

Nigel laughed, and sat up in bed, reaching for his robe, saying, "Brrrr--somewhere warm! How about the south of France? Or maybe the mountains. Annecy is pretty and we could rent a house up the lake. It's lovely. You take a funny little ferry and it stops at all the private jetties to leave the daily cheese, wine and bread order, then gives a little toot on the horn and sets off for the next house. It would be secluded, too. But now we need to get up. You have an appointment with Ootie."

"Oh, yes. And then I need to get the kids and get the ferry home. I'm first in the shower," as she eased slowly out of bed. "I wish we could be together more often. I don't want to leave; I was foolish all those years ago. I should have run away with you when you asked me to."

"Wouldn't have worked. I know that now--we were both too young, too sure of ourselves. We needed to be knocked around emotionally a bit, to take the edges off and make us more accepting, more tolerant. Why won't you divorce Douglas?"

"He says he won't divorce *me*. But anyway, I want to make him pay for what he has done. He stole his brother's work and profited enormously from it, he was unfaithful right from the beginning of our marriage, and he's cruel. Did you know he told me to have an abortion when I was pregnant with Minerva? He made me do all the work to move the family from DC, didn't keep his promises to find somewhere here to live, and started an affair before I even got to Europe. I was an innocent, I believed him when he said he loved me, and I built my life around that."

"Whoa, whoa! Slow down, love! We need to talk about things later, no time now. Get in the shower. Ootie doesn't tolerate lateness."

Thalia's will was drafted and typed quickly in Ootie's chambers. All money and real property to her children, present and future should there be any, as well as the manuscript titled A Family's Pain. Specifically, Douglas Barton, her husband, was excluded from any inheritance. Personal bequests of jewelry, art, furniture and personal items could be added as necessary in subsequent years. She was ushered into an inner sanctum where Ootie himself suggested a further item for her consideration. "Thalia, given the state of your marriage and the importance of the manuscript as you have explained, I think it would be advisable if my firm were authorized to confirm to inquirers that you have indeed made a will and lodged it with us for safekeeping."

Nigel agreed, Thalia consented, and a brief authorization was drafted to be attached to the envelope containing her will. "That way, Douglas will be deterred from any funny business, Thalia, because he'd know it wouldn't help him get hold of the manuscript," Nigel said, "but now that he knows you have it and you understand what it means, he might try to pressure you into giving it up, so you may have to be strong."

Thalia, doubting her strength in opposing Douglas but seeing no other way, agreed and she signed the brief document. Thanking Ootie and his clerk, they left hurriedly to meet Dorrie at the Connaught. In the taxi Thalia and Nigel made their farewells, kissing tenderly and promising to keep in touch daily until it would be possible to be together again.

Dorrie waited impatiently in the hotel foyer, and asked the doorman to bring her car around as soon as possible. "John's coming back unexpectedly tomorrow with a bunch of horses that have to be accommodated in our stables at short notice," she said to Thalia, "I can take you and the kids to Dover, but I have to rush back so let's go."

In the car, Thalia told the whole story of Douglas's unexpected arrival, his forcing her into sex with him, Nigel's reaction, his sister's visit, all the events of that confusing day up to Nigel's presentation of the diamond bangle and her reaction to it. Dorrie listened in silence, softly murmuring sympathy or outrage from time to time, At last Thalia stopped, drew a deep breath, and said "That's it. You know the rest."

"What are you going to do?" asked Dorrie.

"I don't know. I don't want to think about it. I want to tell everyone that I am in love for the first time in my life! I want to shout about it, tell everyone how wonderful it feels, tell them about Nigel and most of all, that he's in love with me!"

"Well!" said Dorrie, "that will be helpful with Douglas, won't it?"

"Alright, Dorrie. I'll calm down. Sorry."

"Nearly there. The children will be happy to see us. Oh, I almost forgot. Cream just had kittens. Do you want one or two? They're Siamese. Let's get the kids together quickly and head for Dover. I rang and warned Cecile and the others, and they should be ready."

"Oooh, yes to the kittens! I'll take them next time I come if they're too small to come now."

The children were playing on the lawns in front of the house. Daniel and the boys were climbing onto a Shetland pony which stood patiently tolerating their noisy rough-and-tumble play while a small pack of large dogs, infected by the energy of the children, raced around barking joyfully. Dorrie's coven of Siamese cats sat in a line on the steps, round blue eyes telegraphing their disapproval of this vulgarity, having forgotten their rowdy kittenhoods. The pony lost patience, bolting away at a smart trot, while Cecile stood on the porch holding a wailing Minerva. "Home sweet home," said Dorrie happily, as she pulled up the car and got out, shouting,

"Redfield, get those dogs under control! Martin and Danny, catch Buttercup and give him a couple of carrots, then all of you go and wash your faces. Hurry up! Move if you want to ride with us to Dover!"

"Oh, Madame!" cried Cecile when she saw Thalia, "I am so glad to see you! I was so worried when Mr. Barton came and said he didn't know where you were."

"My husband was here, Cecile? What did he want?"

"He said he had lost you in London, and that he needed to see you. I told him you are taking us all home on the ferry today, so he went to Dover to wait for us and help us onto the boat. And he said *La Manche* is very calm today and I won't get sick this time, but if I do, he will help me."

Wondering how Douglas could possibly know the weather conditions of the Channel today, and how he planned to help Cecile should she get sick again, Thalia snapped "Cecile, please get Minerva into the car and stay there with her while we round up the boys. If you start crying today I might throw you to the seagulls. *Dépêché-toi*!" and watched as Cecile obediently hurried away with Minnie, pouting with a spoiled teenager expression while the baby gurgled and smiled, amused by the familial chaos surrounding them. And what is Douglas up to, Thalia thought. Turning up here to get information about my movements is sly and sneaky. I'm pretty sure he knew we had ferry reservations for today because I told him when I would be returning and that I would get the car in Ostend and bring it back to Brussels.

Dorrie had the boys in the car now, and called Thalia to come quickly. "No dogs this time. I don't know which is worse, the squabbling dogs or the carsick kids! Or the reverse--carsick dogs and squabbling kids! Sometimes I wonder why I love my life!" She laughed, and Thalia slid into the car quickly; it began to move and Redland, Danny and Cecile started to sing "Alouette", the boys wildly miming the feather-plucking action of the song. "Cecile's teaching them French," said Dorrie, "I'm sure the verb 'to pluck' will be useful in their lives."

The big car eased out of the drive onto the narrow road, the hedges bare now of the summertime tangle of weeds, vines and wildflowers, and Thalia began again to journey into a future not clearly visible to her. Dorrie's contentment in the life that she and John had built for themselves struck a knife blow to her heart. Why are Douglas and I not able to achieve this simple happiness? Is it my fault, am I lacking something that others have? Should I have stayed in Australia with my "tribe"? Is that the trouble? And Nigel? Is that doomed too?

Cecile interrupted her reverie. "*Oooh! Je me sens malade*!" she cried and, adding the action to the words, she opened the window and vomited.

Chapter Thirty-one
Once More Across the Channel

A cold wind was blowing at Dover, there were whitecaps inside the harbor and rough water outside in the Channel. There was no sign of Douglas at the ferry, and as she and Cecile transferred luggage and children from the quay to the indoor cafe of the boat, Thalia thought cynically of his calm weather forecast and promise to Cecile to help her should she get sick.

At last she had people and luggage settled in the noisy cafe, which smelled strongly of fried food and wet wool. Cars and trucks were still being loaded into the vessel's capacious vehicle decks, but Danny and Minerva were sleepy now, and even Cecile looked comfortable enough that Thalia pulled her long fluffy knitted scarf around her neck and shoulders and went on deck to watch their departure from the harbor. On her previous channel crossings, she had enjoyed the sight of the white chalk cliffs which were such a striking element of the coast of the English Channel. They were beloved by the British people who remembered Vera Lynn's version of the song, "There'll Be Bluebirds Over The White Cliffs of Dover" which had done so much to buoy wartime morale. The cliffs were clearly visible as the ship rounded the stone wall surrounding the harbor, but the rough water of the Channel was also visible and daunting to her hopes for a calm crossing.

Peering from the outer deck through the salt-stained glass of the cafe's windows, she could see her little party, still seeming comfortable and not in need of her, and decided to walk a little further toward the stern of the vessel away from the windows of the salon to where she could see a flock of seabirds circling and diving around something in the water. Their harsh cries were blown toward her from the rear by the wind. As she came closer to the birds she leaned over the rail trying to see what was attracting them in the water. Suddenly Douglas emerged from the shelter of a nearby lifeboat stanchion and grabbed her violently, shaking her as he spoke through gritted teeth, "You think you can threaten me, do you? Well, I'll show you. Didn't expect me to be here, did you?"

She attempted to pull away from him but he held her brutally hard against the rigid metal rail. Screaming the words, she said, "Douglas, you're hurting me. Let go of me!" but immediately realized that the shrieks and cries of the birds prevented her voice from being heard by anyone who might be nearby.

"Don't bother screaming," he said, "the birds are making enough noise that noone will hear you. A guy on the quay gave me some fish guts to throw into the water to attract them because I said I like to watch them. Nobody would even notice you in the water while they're kicking up such a fuss. We need to talk."

He began to drag her along the rail toward a corner where there was a small opening between the rail and a metal structure. The opening was not large, but she feared he was going to try to push her overboard by bracing himself against the structure and using leverage to lift her enough that she would be tipped over the rail by her own weight.

"Well, I am not going to talk to someone who is holding me like this. Let me go and I will consider it."

Slowly he released the tight grip he had on her arms, continuing to hold her firmly but more gently. "Behave yourself and I'll let go. I want my manuscript. Where is it?"

"It's not yours, and I am not going to give it to you. And I won't tell you where it is, except that it's safe from you." Her heart was slowing down now as the fear receded, but she realized that Douglas was desperate now that he knew she had the manuscript, and that she had been in real danger.

"I could throw you overboard, Thalia, and I would get everything you have. And no-one would know I did it. No-one knows I'm on board. It would be counted as an accident '*rough seas, leaned over a bit too far, big wave took her. Terrible shame. Husband and children devastated.*'"

"How did you get on board without going through customs and immigration?"

"Easy, these days. The Common Market regs are pretty casual. All I needed was a white shirt, a clipboard, and this hat--bought it in the Bon Marché..." pointing to an officer's peaked-brim hat on the bench nearby, "and nobody looked twice at me as I directed cars onto the parking decks. I'll get off the same way."

"I've made a will, Douglas. Your brother's manuscript is in it. If I die, you will get nothing. And suspicion will fall on you, for sure."

"I don't believe you. You're not that smart."

"Maybe not but I have smart friends. I won't let you see my will, but a solicitor's firm is holding it and is authorized to confirm that to you that it exists."

"What do you want, Thalia?"

Interpreting this as acceptance and temporary surrender, she said "You said you won't divorce me. OK. I don't want a divorce. I want us to stay together until the children get older. It will be less expensive for you if you don't have to maintain two houses, and if we stay together it will keep the gossip down. You can have as many affairs as you want--I assume Beryl and Clemence will eventually be replaced by younger candidate, and you and I will have no marital relations. In other words, no sex with me, especially since you just tried to kill me."

"Think you're in the driver's seat, don't you, little Thalia? You can't prove anything!" he sneered. "And what else?"

"Maybe I can't prove it," she said, "but I won't forget it." She took a deep breath and launched unsmiling into her list. "I can travel whenever I want. I would like a month off from house and kids every year, and occasional weekends too. I want a cat. One of Dorrie's Siamese has just had kittens, and I can have one of them. Or maybe two--one for each child. Or maybe three--one for me too. And I have a plan to start a small business, and I hope you won't raise objections."

"I suppose you want my financial help with that?"

"Are you offering? I won't refuse. You've made enough with your brother's book that you can spare a bit for me. You can let go of me now, I'm cold. I need to pull up my scarf."

He released his grip on her reluctantly, “It’s my book. He was dumb and careless, not to safeguard it. What’s this great business opportunity?”

“An agency to help new people get settled in Brussels.” Thalia was grateful for the fluffy scarf around her shoulders; it gave her a moment to think as she rearranged it against the windy chill. The wind was stronger now as the ship nosed ponderously into the waves. A channel ferry is not the most graceful of vessels, she thought. “Where to find a real estate agent who speaks your language, how much to pay the cleaning lady, a list of plumbers, electricians and gardeners who won’t try to rob you, English-speaking medical people, best nursery schools, where to find the ‘little dressmaker’ that all the chic Belgian ladies seem to have, all the things that I am having to learn for myself. Maintain lists, charge for consultations, introduce people at small elegant gatherings, and even maybe a London extension that Dorrie would handle.”

Douglas looked at her appraisingly, “Could work, Thalia. How much would you need to begin?” Surprised, she wondered if Douglas could be turned into an ally, even an unwilling one?

If he offers money and support, he is giving tacit approval to my whole plan, she thought. But if I accept his money, I ally myself with him, and give my approval to his theft of

Peter's book, and to his lame attempt to kill me. I don't like that, but I think I need to take the money. I can work my way to independence, and if it's successful, perhaps I can leave Douglas, take care of the children and have my own life. With Nigel. "Not sure yet. I can work up a plan when we get home."

But I have another problem, one that I am not able to make a plan for. If I am to give Nigel the child he wants from me, I will have to sleep with Douglas sometimes, at least until I conceive, at least if I want to stay with him. I will have to deceive him into believing the child is his. And how can I be sure that it *is* Nigel's child? So much for my declaration of "no sex with me." As for ethical considerations, he should have thought of those before he began his affairs. I guess I need to rethink this whole thing.

"Did that tight-arsed English guy with the long hair put you up to this? Are you in bed with him? I challenged him to a duel, you know, but he was chicken. What can he do that I can't?"

"Be kind. And truthful." Just like I am, she thought, mocking herself. "Do we have an agreement?"

Douglas sighed. His face softened a little, and he at last released his hold on her arms. "Yes, we have an agreement. You know, I really thought we had a chance when we met in Australia. I liked your independence, your thoughtful way of approaching life. I even liked your crazy cat. For a while, it was good, wasn't it? Those first years in Alexandria, our little house? I'm sorry."

She didn't answer immediately. She was pensive when she did respond. "Yes, those years were good. Right up through the weekend in Tidewater when Minerva was conceived. The candlelight dinners in the garden in that terrible DC humidity, my feeling that our marriage was secure after that weekend, that your affairs were over. But it all fell apart. When you told me to have an abortion, something changed in me, and I can't forget it. But let's not talk about that part of it. It's history. She's here. No use revisiting it. I'll try not to be bitter."

He laughed. "You know me. I am what I am, you know what you're getting. Can you cope with this setup? And what about the kids? Have you thought about them?"

"Of course I have. What do you take me for? I plan to go away for a month each year, dates established in advance, with a nanny brought in to help care for them. It would give you time to bond with them both, get to know them, and let them know you. I'll miss them, but I think it will be good for them to be a bit more independent as they grow up. And I am sure Dorrie can give me recommendations for a reliable, capable person."

“Who are you going with? And where are you planning to go?”

“I won’t answer. No questions asked or answered. These are my conditions for keeping quiet about your brother’s manuscript. Take it or leave it.”

Slowly, he said, “I don’t seem to have an alternative.” He had given up too easily, she knew. It’s not over, but I’ll take it for now.

“We will need a bigger house with more bedrooms.” she said.

Cecile appeared on the deck. “*Oh, Madame! Je veux Maman! Et aussi de l’eau de Vichy!*”

As she headed to the rail, Thalia yelled at her. “Not into the wind, Cecile! Get the wind behind you!” But it was too late.

Chapter Thirty-two

The House on Avenue Molière, 1973

The water calmed as the ferry entered the harbor at Ostend, but Cecile didn't. "I tell you, Madame, I never will go to boat again. Nevernevernever! *Fiche moi la paix! Je m'en fiche.* I quit, Madame. I home to go."

Thalia, thinking that it might be a good idea if Cecile did indeed go home since she was of so little use, helped her clean herself while Douglas dealt with the children and the luggage. Well, she thought, at least *he's* being useful right now, but I wonder how long it will last. They trailed off the ship onto the quay, Thalia leading with Danny holding her hand, Douglas lagging, issuing loud commands to the porter and pushing Minerva in the stroller, and Cecile far behind as if unwilling to be seen with them.

"I'll get the car from the hotel, Thalia," Douglas bellowed, "You and Cecile wait here with Danny and the luggage. Minnie'll be fine with me." We look like a happy family, Thalia thought, no problems except how to get the family and the luggage into the car after a long weekend in London. Well, we'll see what happens when we get home.

The charming house in Watermael Boitsfort at the edge of the Forêt de Soignes seemed very small now. Cecile unpacked the children's things while Thalia moved her belongings to the bedroom currently occupied by Daniel, leaving the big bedroom to Douglas. He said nothing as she worked at moving her clothes, neither did he offer to help. When she had finished, he said, "You're really going through with this then, Thalia?"

"Yes. I will be looking for a larger house as soon as I can. Do you have a preference for location?"

"Not really. I'm leaving for Paris tomorrow, and I will probably be there for the next few months anyway. Suit yourself, just be sure there's enough space so that we don't have to move again."

So Thalia engaged again with Mademoiselle Florence and Madame Rennes, promising the latter that she would find another tenant for the little house as soon as she could get her new agency running, and that Douglas would cover the rent until that could be arranged. The price of spending time with your mistress in Paris, Douglas, she thought. By contrast with her arrival some months ago, she was now familiar with the districts of Brussels and decided to concentrate on Avenue Moliére, a tree-lined street in the Ixelles district, where there were a number of large houses and numerous "*Maison à Louer*" signs in the street level windows. Florence agreed to inspect them and choose the two most likely to be suitable for the Bartons. Cecile would stay with the family until the summer, she said, if she were not required to go near a boat, thus allowing Thalia time to prepare a business plan to present to Douglas for funding for her new venture.

Can I trust Douglas? This thought kept coming back to her as she worked. Why has he accepted this situation so calmly, almost placidly? What is he up to? No word came from Paris, no telephone calls, no inquiries about the welfare of family at home, just a long and perhaps ominous silence. Was Clemence so beguiling still?

She finished her business plan and sent it to him, stressing that costs would be lessened if the new house were to have a room suitable for an office, and not mentioning that she planned to defray many of the start-up costs from her own account should he decide to be stingy with his money. Thalia had been careful with the money in the account she had established when selling the house in Alexandria, and it had accumulated a little but she preferred to keep it as security for her and the children, so she would use it now only if necessary. The plan she was submitting to Douglas was frugal, so perhaps she could use some of her money for the little feminine touches that would help to bring in clients.

Florence reported that she had inspected several of the houses on Avenue Molière and found only one that was suitable for the family. But, she noted, it was a fine residence, suitable for a gentleman's family and large enough for all of them, with an office and coat room on the street level and several handsome reception rooms above. Thalia asked Florence to make a reservation for her to inspect the premises the next day, and since the rain had stopped, took a walk to the nearby park with Danny riding his tricycle beside her and Minerva in the stroller.

As she neared home on her way back, she heard Cecile calling from the garden "Madame! Madame! Mr. Barton is *au telefon! Dépêchez-vous, s'il vous plait!",* and Thalia began to hurry. Why is Douglas calling? I haven't heard a word from him for two weeks, since he left us here when we got back from London.

"Thalia? Douglas here" he said, as if she might not recognize his voice. "Well, I can lend you the money. I'll have my attorney draw up a loan agreement for you to sign."

"A loan? How generous of you, are you sure I am good for it, Douglas? Might be a risk, can't be too careful with your money."

"Sarcasm doesn't suit you, Thalia. I've told you that before."

Thalia decided to let that one pass. It was a favorite insult of his, anyway. "Well, thank you. I think it's a good plan."

Douglas responded, "It looks promising. I ran it by a friend and she agrees that it would be very useful. There is some support of this kind now but it's mostly nationality-specific--i.e., British help British, Dutch Dutch, and so on. If you can cross the international barrier, you could have a big audience."

The friend was probably Clemence, thought Thalia. Nice of her to be supportive of my plan. I wonder whether she knows that Douglas and I have reached an understanding, and that he's free to play the field now. Well, not to worry. Decisions made, no looking back. And she could go forward with her plan, already well into the development phase.

The house on tree-lined Avenue Molière was perfect for their needs. Tall, narrow but deep, it was in the Brussels style of the early twentieth century with bay windows bringing as much of the soft northern light as possible to the large rooms, polished wood parquet floors, and marble mantels on the fireplaces. A small *art nouveau* skylight above the staircase charmed Thalia with its spangled drops of colored light on sunny days. There were five floors: *rez de chausée*, first, second and third floors, with five generous bedrooms and three bathrooms, and a small *au pair* suite in the attic. The *rez de chausée*, a little below street level, had a large entrance hall, a separate office and coat room, and a kitchen with windows to the enclosed rear garden. There was no elevator. Good exercise, thought Thalia but reflected that it was revealing of the importance of good food to Belgians that a dumbwaiter supplied quick food service from the kitchen to the salon on the first floor and the dining room on the second floor while the people who prepared and served it had to climb the stairs. The rear windows overlooked the private garden, currently an unkempt tangle of vines and overgrown shrubs providing shelter for a multitude of birds, but sunny and promising possibilities for flowers.

The house, like the garden, was a little shabby and in need of attention. The office on the entry level is perfect, she thought, for the headquarters of my new agency, and the house itself will be an impressive setting for events to introduce new residents to Brussels.

Thalia signed the lease for the house, the *etat de lieu* was completed, and she and the children settled in, pleased with the new space but regretful that they had to leave the warm charm of the little house at the edge of the great forest. Douglas remained in Paris during the move, offering scant encouragement by telephone although he did send the money needed for the deposit. Thalia had his belongings boxed by the movers and put in one of the bedrooms of the new house for him to arrange when he returned. For herself, she reserved the largest of the bedrooms with its luxurious attached bathroom, and a view of the garden.

And so began the longest period of contentment Thalia had ever known.

Beginning that year, she and Nigel passed a month together every summer, choosing quiet secluded places in warm climates where Nigel, who was acquiring fame as an actor, might not be recognized. A favorite place was the small French town of Annecy in the Haute Savoie where the water of the lake was fed by streams from the glaciers above, supplying water clear and transparent as the mountain air. The white swans glided regally, barely rippling the surface but in the clear water one could see their large webbed feet paddling furiously below, belying the effortless grace of their movements on the surface.

In 1973, their first summer together, Nigel rented a house for them on the side of the mountain, looking down at a village at the edge of Lake Annecy. From their verandah, they could watch the progress of the ferry bringing supplies from the town, packed and loaded onto the boat in Annecy--the twice-daily fresh bread, crisp lettuce from the town's fields, milk, butter and cheese from the dairy herds which spent their summers in the mountain fields, Cavaillon melons and tender *poulets de Bresse,* all the simple exquisite foods of France. And plastic containers of wine from the local *cave cooperatif,* where the vintners of the area brought their wines to be blended with others to make the district's *vin ordinaire*. The housekeeper brought their supplies daily from the ferry, driving her tiny *Citroën,* the market basket of French housewives.

To make this idyll possible, Thalia engaged the services of Mrs. Hobson, highly recommended by Dorrie, whose experience with nannies was unsurpassed in the south of England. Nigel deposited a generous sum of money in Thalia's business account to be used to pay Mrs. Hobson, and Douglas was none-the-wiser as to who was paying this bill. Mrs. Hobson's old-fashioned firmness and kindness pleased the children, and Thalia was comfortable in leaving them for a month.

The relationship between Thalia and Nigel deepened during these weeks, ripening into a satisfying and comforting partnership. Nigel rented a little motorboat in which they could explore the lakes in the area, spending their days picnicking under trees on the grassy banks of the water, or sometimes venturing on foot up to the high pastures where the village herds were taken for the summer. On days when the mountain fog and mist filled the valleys, they lit a fire in the fireplace in the living room and spent the day reading or listening to music from the collection of old vinyl records in the corner where the old-fashioned record player lived, often ending the day with joyful lovemaking.

Thalia had never been so happy, she thought. In all the years with Douglas she had never experienced the joy that she felt every day she spent with Nigel.

Chapter Thirty-three

Avenue Molière, 1974--2005

Thalia's third child, Diana, was born in Brussels in April of 1974. Daniel, Minerva and Diana were brought up together in the Avenue Molière house, attending the small private school in the neighborhood which catered to the children of the wealthy community. Instruction was in French and, as required by Belgian law at the time, with some classes in Flemish, the other official language of the country. English was spoken at home, and the Barton children became bilingual in French and English.

The children flourished, although very different in personality and temperament. Sunny Minerva was the peacemaker of the family, while Daniel, gregarious and fun-loving, delighted in teasing his sisters, sometimes making the dramatic and sensitive Diana cry and storm out of the room. They all though adapted easily to Belgian customs, walking or bicycling to school and riding the city buses to such extra-curricular activities as Boy and Girl Scouts, football, tennis, piano and dance lessons, the usual occupations of middle-class children everywhere.

To Thalia's surprise, Douglas participated enthusiastically in the social life of *Comme Chez Soi,* becoming a warm and welcoming host, and a sought-after guest at many private events. She though found it difficult to trust him completely, and preferred not to include him in the financial details of the organization as far as possible. He brought much useful inside knowledge of the upper echelons of European bureaucracy, probably acquired, she suspected, from his numerous romantic entanglements. Clemence had long ago been supplanted by others, and Thalia no longer bothered to remember their names, if she even heard them at all.

Comme Chez Soi flourished. After two years, Thalia had paid off the loan from Douglas and became independent of his financial control. Two years after that, she purchased the house in her own name and engaged more staff. Fashionable well-do-do Brussels ladies flocked to the coffee mornings, afternoon teas, and cocktail gatherings held there. Ambassadors' wives poured tea from gleaming silver teapots, and smilingly passed the milk and sugar. It was possible to arrange private events, with exclusive guest lists and costly catered food service ordered by Thalia's staff. Small wedding events could be accommodated too, and *Comme Chez Soi* brought many formerly unknown American customs to Brussels--rehearsal dinners, bridesmaids' lunches, box lunches for picnics in the garden, as well as traditional children's birthday parties with clowns, and intimate dinners in the candlelit dining room.

Thalia and Douglas separated in 1980, but he continued to refuse to divorce her. She realized that their marriage provided him with a comfortable refuge against any pressure for commitment from his extramarital partners and, since she still felt that Nigel needed to remain free and untrammelled by legal ties, she accepted the situation and was glad that Douglas had gone out of her life to the extent that he had done. He agreed that the children should remain in her care, and she was happy that he did not attempt to get control of them. Under the Napoleonic Code of Belgian law, it might have proved difficult for her to keep them if he had chosen to make trouble for her. Altogether, it was a moderately amicable separation.

Thalia and the files of *Comme Chez Soi* constituted the institutional social memory of Brussels and the official organizations headquartered in the city--NATO and the Common Market, as well as the many large international corporations which had gathered there because of the concentration of power. She and her staff were familiar with the restaurants of the city, the places of historical interest, schedules of trains, buses and airports, the numerous elementary and high schools, and the comings and goings of the country's politicians and society people. Newcomers to the city were given the telephone number and the address and advised to talk to someone there for help with almost any lawful service they might need. Under Thalia's strict control, the staff worked with discretion. *Comme Chez Soi* staff may have heard the gossip, but they were forbidden to pass it on.

Thalia received a diagnosis of cancer in 2001 and was forced to retire; the news flashed through the international community almost in minutes. Her daughter Minerva attempted to continue the business, and succeeded in doing so for a year but eventually Thalia decided to close it down and dismiss the staff. The spacious rooms of the gracious house fell silent. Thalia and Minerva continued to live there, two of the blue-eyed Siamese cats remained, descendants of long-ago Butter and Jam, and could be seen from time to time sleeping in a patch of sun or sitting in a window watching the world go by in the street outside. Daniel and Diana, grown now and building their own lives, lived in apartments nearby and came frequently to help their mother and sister.

Nigel came to visit, but the summer trips were no more. Douglas, living now in Brussels but on the other side of the city, remained in touch but remotely and without warmth. His relationship with the children had never been much more than cordial, lacking the love that should have endeared them to him, and vice versa. In her most private thoughts, Thalia knew that she had been mistaken in marrying him. She had been too young, too inexperienced in life, as Amelia had told her although perhaps not in the way that Amelia had meant. She had lacked sexual experience certainly, but more importantly she had not known what might have helped to open communications between Douglas and herself to work toward solutions. Had she been responsible in any way for his infidelities, she wondered. Could she have changed anything? Did the failure of her marriage define her life? Or was her life defined by the longtime and ongoing infidelity with Nigel?

The cancer treatments, at first encouraging, became less effective and at last Thalia's doctors admitted that they could do no more. Hospice services, a new and innovative way to help with the end of life by bringing people out of the restrictive hospital setting and placing them at home, were engaged and Thalia was able to return to her own bedroom where she could be surrounded by her belongings, and where the two cats were free to pass the days with her. She had long ago abandoned her custom of using food names for them; these two, mother and daughter, were named Nefertiti and Meret, but mostly answered to Neffie and Mettie. As cats sometimes do, they adopted the role of nurse and one or both could usually be found curled up on the bed with Thalia, or sleeping somewhere in her room.

And so, the beginning of the end for Thalia.

Chapter Thirty-four

Thalia, 2005

“The nurse says Mother won’t last the night, Diana, so you need to get here ASAP,” Minerva told her sister on the phone from their mother’s hospice room. “I'll call Daniel now and tell him too."

"Oh, so soon! I thought she would have more time. I’m not dressed yet. Had a late night last night. A new man in my life!”

Minerva sighed. Her sister hated to hurry, couldn’t seem to do it, apparently not even in order to be with her mother on her deathbed. “Diana, you need to get a wriggle on. You can tell me about the new man later and get on the road now, for goodness’ sake!” She hung up, exasperated, and called their brother Daniel, older than she by four years. “Danny, hospice nurse says Mother’s on the edge, probably won’t make it to morning.”

“I’ll be there as soon as I can,” he said, as Minerva began to cry. “Hang in there, love,” he said gently.

“Thanks, Dan. And… could you call Dad too, please? I just don’t want to have to deal with him today.” Her voice wavering, and still on the edge of tears, hardly hearing her brother's words of reassurance, she continued, "he seems to think Mother's dying is an act of hostility designed to inconvenience him!"

"I'll deal with him, Minnie, just focus on Mother right now." As she disconnected from his call, she looked at her mother sleeping in the hospital bed, pale and thin but retaining much of her beauty. The cancer that was taking her hadn't marked her outwardly, except for the loss of her hair. Shoulder-length and auburn to the end, helped along by expensive treatments and care from skilled hairdressers, it had been both her distinguishing feature and her vanity. Now, after refusing a wig, she wore a silk scarf twisted around her head to cover the stark baldness of end-stage cancer.

Minerva looked around the room, glad that they had been able to arrange for hospice care at home for Thalia. Although the sunny room had been stripped of many of its furnishings in order to provide space for the nurses and family who maintained care for the dying woman, it was still full of the personality of the woman who inhabited it. The books in the shelves spoke of her wide-ranging interests in art, music and literature, while the collection of gardening and cook books were reminders of her domestic side. Minerva thought of the family dinners with their eclectic menus reflecting her mother's current interests in the cuisine of some exotic land--Java perhaps, or Mali, or a long-ago enthusiasm for the cuisine of Indian hill tribes, brought to a sharp conclusion by difficulty in getting the exotic ingredients and objections from the family to those ingredients when they were obtained.

The door of the room opened quietly and a nurse entered. "Is the family on the way?" she asked, then, "When they get here, could you come out and talk to me?" Minerva nodded, and as Nurse Berry left the room, Thalia opened her eyes and turned her head toward her daughter.

Softly she said, “Minnie darling, I’m glad you’re here. I don’t think I can hold on much longer. Is your father coming? There’s something in my things for him."

"They're all on the way, Mama, Dad too, I think. Diana has a new love interest. Up too late last night.”

The two women laughed, and Thalia said, "Oh, first things first with Diana! I do wish she would settle down and get married. She leads such a pointless life.” She moved restlessly, trying to find a comfortable position.

"Are you in pain, Mama?" Minerva asked. "The nurse can give you more morphine, if you are."

"No, no more just now. I want to be clear in my mind. Next time I go to sleep, I will sleep for a long time."

Minerva caught her mother's meaning and, trying not to show her distress, said "Oh, Mama! What do you need that I can do?"

"Well, you can help me to sit up a bit, and give me that silly lace bed jacket that Helene gave me. Does she think I'm Elizabeth Barrett Browning, a Victorian invalid, languishing beautifully? And you can fetch my jewelry box from the shelf in the armoire, please."

"Oh, Mama! Helene just wanted to give you something pretty! She's such a dear friend! And you must admit that it IS pretty!" She rummaged around and found the bedjacket, a lacy pink confection, and helped her mother into it, then went to the armoire for the jewelry box. Shoebox-sized, it was covered with dark blue Italian leather printed with tiny bunches of pink and blue flowers. As she carried it to the bedside, she reflected that none of Thalia's children had been allowed to open the box, ever. Not for them the fun of rummaging through the shiny things in it, choosing their favorites and claiming them for the future. They had, of course, seen items from it when their mother wore them--the aquamarine earrings the color of her eyes, the heavy gold bangle with the solitaire diamond, and the native American turquoise and silver necklace and earrings she wore almost daily.

"Just put it here on the bed next to me, Minnie. I want to look at it with you and the others. I wish they would hurry!"

Her voice was whispery now; she sounded fretful and anxious, and her hands were twisting the flimsy edges of the bed jacket so hard that Minerva thought the fabric might tear. "There's something I want your father to see too, when we're all together."

The quiet of the room was shattered as the door flew open with a bang and in, on a gust of bluster and noise, came Douglas Caldwell, estranged husband of Thalia and father of her children. "Need some attention, do you, Thalia?" he boomed. "Everybody neglecting you? Well, here we all are," then pausing to look around," or will be when Diana gets away from her latest crush and Daniel the Peacekeeper gets here."

"Dad, please don't! This isn't the time. Mama needs peace now." Minerva looked at her mother as she said this, and seeing that Thalia's eyes were filled with tears, moved to sit protectively by the bed. "Mama, what do you need? What can I do?"

"Just what you said. I need peace. Douglas, please, for once in your life think about someone other than yourself! Can't you just sit down and behave properly?"

Douglas sat down heavily on the fragile sofa across the room from Thalia's bed. "I don't know how to behave properly in the circumstances. Will this do?" he queried as he folded his hands together on his lap and adopted an exaggerated expression of sadness. "I hate this room," he said, in a polite conversational tone, "I always feel like a bull in a china shop in here. All this female delicacy, insipid colors, it's too *dainty*."

Thalia, even in extremis, was capable of reacting to this old canard from Douglas. "Well," she snapped, "you haven't spent much time in here anyway for a long time now."

"By mutual agreement, dearest!" said her husband. "Ahh, here are my other offspring," as Daniel and Diana entered. "Well, well. Daniel, carrier into the future of the proud family name! And Diana, Girl About Town, aspiring theatrical star. Pity you seem to lack talent, the essential."

Diana, already upset and emotional, flushed with anger at his mocking tone, her eyes filling with tears. "Dad, you know very well there's not much opportunity here, but I'm building my skills, getting noticed. I'd do better in London but you won't give me the money," she said. Then, beginning to cry, ran to her mother and hugged her as Thalia stroked her hair gently. Saying, "I love you, Mama", she moved a little to make room for Daniel too to come close to Thalia. The three sat quietly together, with eyes and loving touch sending unspoken messages from their hearts.

Hoping to forestall another sarcastic remark from Douglas, Minerva moved to pick up the jewelry box and took it to her mother, asking “Do you want this now, Mama?” Her brother and sister jumped up to make room for the box, then clustered with Minerva on the end of the bed.

“Prizegiving time now, is it? Distributing all that pretty stuff I bought you?" Douglas asked brusquely, perhaps a little moved by the tender scene he had just witnessed, although perhaps not. Tenderness wasn't his *forte*.

“Not yet, Douglas. Something I want to show you first but the pain is getting worse. Minnie, could you call the nurse for pain relief, please?" The others, looking worried, turned toward Minerva who, saying she would call the nurse, left the room. Nurse Berry was waiting in the hall, and said, "I heard her ask for pain relief now, and I can give it to her but I think you should know that there's a risk that the morphine dose necessary to suppress the pain will depress her breathing, and she may die. This is what I wanted to tell you when you arrived."

"Does she know this?"

"Yes. She knows and understands. We have talked about it recently. As you know, in her living will she gave you legal authority to make this decision for her. Do you agree to this?"

Minerva said, "Should I ask the others?"

"It would prolong her pain."

Leaning against the wall, Minerva said, "Can I sit down for a moment? I don't think I can stand right now." But then, straightening, she said, "Of course, I must. Yes, please do it."

As she and the nurse re-entered the room, all eyes turned toward her. Going to her mother's bedside, she motioned to the family to gather round. As Nurse Berry administered the morphine, they held hands. Unnoticed, the nurse left the room as Diana, with her warm soprano voice, began quietly to sing a favorite song of Thalia's, and one by one the others joined in. Thalia very softly sang the first few bars, but gradually her voice faded, her breathing slowed, and she was gone.

2005

Chapter Thirty-five

Chagrin d'amour

The house on Avenue Molière, four days later

The late afternoon sun sent shafts of cool spring light falling across the room where Thalia died. Restored now to its usual appearance, the hospital bed where Thalia had spent her last days gone and her large luxurious bed restored to its place, it was a peaceful setting for the family which had gathered to read her will and distribute the things she had bequeathed to them. Her jewelry box sat on the long table between the deep windows, and there were several additional chairs now in a group with the little sofa.

Minerva spoke quietly..."Di, I thought your song was lovely and I think Mama approved too. I was surprised that she sang along, but she loved to sing, didn't she? Remember all those car trips when we were kids? The pile of songbooks in the back seat?"

"What made you choose to sing, Diana?" asked Daniel, from the window seat where he could see Thalia's garden, late daffodils and tulips in bloom. Tall and lanky, auburn-haired like his mother, his voice carried a hint of hers with its faint accent and inflection. "And that song in particular?"

"I remembered how much we all sang together, like Minnie said, and how happy those trips together were. You don't approve of that song, Danny?" asked his younger sister.

"No, it's lovely, but the words are sad... *'Plaisir d'amour, ne dure qu'un instant, chagrin d'amour dure toute la vie-* -the pleasure of love lasts for only a moment, but the sadness of love lasts for a lifetime' – do you think she believed that? "

"Perhaps," said Diana. "Life with Dad wasn't filled with romance. I'd like to get this over with. It's hard being in this room without her... it was so much HER place, wasn't it? I wish Dad would get here so we can get things moving."

"You called, Di?" answered Douglas, entering at that moment. "Here I am. Do we have to be in here? I don't like this room. But, OK if you want it. Let's get down to business and see what's in the box." He seemed hostile, a little more keyed up than the situation required, Minerva thought and wondered why. Did he really care about Thalia's death? They'd been separated for years. "Who'll do the honors?"

"It should be Minnie," replied Diana, "she's Mama's executor." Agreement was quick, and Minerva, taking the box from the table where it rested, sat down on the sofa. Daniel and Diana moved to join her, but Douglas distanced himself by moving to the window seat vacated by Daniel.

With Thalia's will in her hand, Minerva opened the box. The family leaned in to look, with the exception of Douglas who, apparently bored, rested languidly in the window seat and stared out the window. No sparkle of jewels greeted their gaze, just neatly stacked velvet boxes, some small and round, others square, still others long and shallow. Minerva, checking the will's list, lifted out the first box and opened it, revealing the aquamarine earrings her mother had worn so often. "This is to go to me, together with the matching ring." she said, and set it aside.

Diana began to cry. "Oh, I really wanted that ring! Why didn't she give *me* that?"

Douglas, rousing from his window-gazing, said, "For heaven's sake, Diana, get a grip and stop being a baby! I gave those earrings to her when we were first married! But I didn't know there was a ring. She must have bought that for herself. Odd thing to do. I would have bought it if she had told me she wanted it."

Next came a deep sea-green box containing a heavy gold bangle with a solitaire diamond. "This one's for you, Diana," said Minerva, handing the box to her sister. "I've always loved that bangle. Aren't you lucky?" Diana stopped crying and smiled with pleasure. Douglas muttered a little about not remembering the bangle, but remained quiet.

She continued distributing the jewelry until the box was empty, except for a flat brown envelope on the very bottom. "She told me there was something she wanted you to see, Dad. Maybe this is it" she said, pulling out the unsealed envelope and opening it. "Oh, look--it's a little photo album!"

Daniel took it from her hand and began to leaf through it. "I don't recognize any of the people except Mama. The first photo is dated 1965. It's a group. They look very chic, very London... the background looks like shipboard. A cruise, perhaps. It's black and white, looks like the ones ships' photographers used to take."

Looking over Daniel's shoulder, Diana said, "I wonder if it was when she left Australia the first time? She was only 25, and she looks about that in the photo. I wonder who the other people are?"

"Let's see how many photos there are, total" said Daniel, turning pages rapidly to look at the date written on the lower part of the page. "Looks like one about every year or so for a long time, up till last year."

"Let's see the next one, Danny!" said Minerva. Daniel handed her the little book and she flipped to the next page, and said "This one's dated 1980. It's in color..." Her voice slowed as she realized the possible implications of this photograph, showing a man and a woman seated together at a table beneath a gaily colored umbrella, his arm encircling her shoulders and pulling her close to him. The woman, the mature Thalia, her thick auburn hair pulled back to frame her delicate face, smiled confidently into the camera.

Diana, seated close to her sister, said "His face is somehow familiar, you know. I feel as if I've seen him before. Is he in all the pictures, Minnie?"

"... not sure. Looks like it though, but older of course. Just him and Mama!" replied Minerva. "Ummm...maybe these aren't for Dad, I don't know."

Douglas had been silent over on the windows seat up until now but, hearing this, he jumped up and looked at the first photo, then tried to snatch the album from Minerva's hand. She held onto it stubbornly. "This is for me!" he shouted, trying to gain control of it but Minerva managed to pull it out of his reach. "It's none of your business! Give it to me NOW!" he ordered. "And there should be something else too. Are you hiding things from me?"

"No, I'm not hiding anything. This is the only thing I didn't expect to find. Everything else in the jewelry box is in her will. Dad, it wasn't marked with your name and there is nothing in the will about it. Mama made me executor, and I need to investigate this before I give it to you." Not sure of her legal ground, Minerva decided that Douglas wouldn't know either, so she took the risk. "I'll ask the attorney about it, and give it to you if he says it's alright."

The doorbell rang, loud in the silence of the house, and Douglas subsided, quiet but grumbling under his breath. With Thalia's illness and death the bustling social life of her home had ended. It had been a long time now since the light notes of women's laughter and the clinking of delicate china and silver had brightened the mornings. No longer did the door from Avenue Molière swing open to admit the fashionably dressed wives of diplomats and high level bureaucrats, generals and admirals from SHAPE and NATO, or executives of international corporations. No children played on the swings in the enclosed garden, and only two blue-eyed Siamese cats remained to bask on the sun-warmed stones outside the back door. Almost all the atmosphere of gaiety and friendship was gone now, since the discovery of the cancer which took her life.

"Who on earth?" said Minerva, displeased by this distraction. "I suppose I will have to go, there's no-one else here today." She left the room and the others could hear her descending the long staircase to the ground level. The voices from the foyer were inaudible to those in the bedroom, but at last they could hear Minerva returning with a companion. As she entered, she said, "I know this is a surprise, everyone. This gentleman was directed to come today by Sir Outerbridge Ripley, Mama's attorney in London. I will let him introduce himself."

The newcomer, a handsome man with dark hair greying at the temples, not young but aging gracefully, stood in the doorway smiling, hesitating a little before he spoke, his air of diffidence balanced by the charm in his voice and smile. "Hello, Thalia's family! I'm an old friend of your mother..."

He stopped, brusquely interrupted by Douglas who, bristling, charged up and stood close to the visitor, challenging him. "I know who you are, Somerville! Haven't had the nerve to show up in front of me for a long time, have you? I remember you. Too cowardly to accept my challenge, weren't you? And what are you doing here today trespassing on our grief?"

Nigel Somerville, smiling faintly, replied, "I'm flattered that you remember me, Douglas, but I recall that challenge a little differently. You seemed a bit less enthusiastic about it after you heard about my shooting awards at Cambridge, didn't you?" He stepped away from Douglas, moving toward the window. "But I'm not here to joust with you. I came to meet Thalia's family, and I seem to have arrived at an awkward time." Turning to the children, he asked "May I come back in an hour or so, after you have finished your remembrances? I wouldn't bother you but it's important."

Douglas shouted sneeringly, "Going to justify you and her sleeping together for so many years, eh? Think I didn't know?" Turning to the others, he snarled, "yeah, she was a slut. Slept with this prick whenever she got the chance... a month every summer for years! Didn't you wonder where she went every summer?" Since they had indeed wondered that, it was hard to ignore the question but Daniel broke in.

"Dad, stop. Don't talk about Mama that way! Shut up and leave now, if you can't control yourself. We need to know what this man wants to tell us. He says it's important." He turned to his sisters and asked, "Do you agree?" Silently, they both nodded, and he said "Dad, please go. We'll talk later."

His face cold, he stared at his father until Douglas turned away. "We'll see about this" he blustered "You won't get the truth from him anyway. I'll be back." He stormed out, slamming the door as he went.

The silence was long and heavy, unbroken until Diana spoke. Her voice curt and apparently challenging him, she asked, "I saw you in a play in London last year, Mr. Somerville. How did you know our mother?"

Nigel replied, "You must be Diana. It's a very long story! It's going to take a while, but I think you will want to hear it all. The short version, perhaps, will be enough for today though. But first, I need to present my credentials. May I sit down?" He walked over to the window seat just vacated by Douglas, seating himself in a patch of sun. "I feel know you all from your photos. Minerva, you look very like your mother when I first met her. We were on a ship, the P&O *Oriana*, sailing from Sydney to Vancouver. I had been in Australia working with an acting troupe, and the group was returning to London together. She was going to Vancouver to marry your father."

Minerva asked "Is that you in the photo of the group that was in the little album in her jewelry box?"

"I suppose so. There were a lot of photos taken on board that ship. I was sitting alone on the deck in the dark of midnight on the first night at sea when your mother showed up and began to tell me about the albatross and the Ancient Mariner. I fell in love with her right then. And stayed in love, still am, even though she's gone. I asked her to marry me then, but she said she had promised to marry Douglas. So..."

Daniel interrupted this monologue, saying, "Were you sleeping together like Dad said?"

Nigel sighed, and said, "Yes. That's another part of the story, coming a bit later. You won't like it very much, but I hope you'll understand. In your mother's will, she mentions the manuscript of A Family's Pain, the book published by your father but written by his brother, your uncle, Peter Barton, who died in 1966. Peter sent a copy of it to your mother just before he died, and she has had it in her possession ever since. She left it to her children, as you probably know from the will." Stumbling a little over his words at this part of the story, by contrast with his smooth delivery earlier, he went on. "I find this part of the story difficult to understand and to condone, frankly. She used her knowledge of your father's theft of his brother's work to control him, and to revenge his treatment of her."

Minerva asked, "My first question--there are lots of questions, obviously-- but my first is where is the manuscript now?"

"I have brought it with me. It's in here." He held up a black leather attache case, and standing up, he moved to the table around which they were sitting and laid the case there. Returning to the window seat he said “Thalia borrowed money from your father, and also lived mostly at his expense for years while she built her business. She knew that by taking his money, she was condoning his theft of the manuscript which provided the wealth in which she was sharing. But she wanted revenge for his treatment of her. He was serially unfaithful from the earliest days of their marriage, cruel and careless of her feelings in other ways too.” He paused for a moment, and appeared to be struggling with an impulse to say more, but continued slowly.

"So, something which might figure into your judgments is this: your mother is dead now. Perhaps it’s time to give the manuscript to your father and release him from the threat of exposure that he has had for so long. It’s up to the three of you now. You have a lot to think about. And now, I’ve discharged one part of my duty, I think.”

“But there’s something else that I want to tell you, something which is very personal to me, and far too long delayed.” This time he was obviously nervous, sitting tense and straight on the bench, and his voice trembled a little as he spoke. “Diana, may I see the bangle, please? The gold bangle with the solitaire diamond that your mother specified must go to you?”

Diana looked confused. How could this man know about a piece of her mother's jewelry? "Why? "she asked, "I don't understand. How do you know about the bangle? Why are you so interested in this family?"

"That's a sensible attitude toward a stranger, I suppose, but this time I assure you this stranger can be trusted. The bangle, please?"

His voice carried an intensity of feeling, a desperate plea for understanding, that impressed them all. "Di, it can't hurt to let him see it" said her brother, adding, "Minnie and I are both here. I think it's safe." and Minerva nodded agreement.

Picking up the case containing the bangle, Diana walked over to the window seat where Nigel was sitting and handed it to him. He opened the case and took the piece out; a ray of sun caught the diamond, sending tiny rainbows around the room and making Diana say "Oh! How pretty!"

"The stone is from my grandmother's engagement ring," said Nigel, facing Diana and appearing to speak to her alone. "I had the bracelet made and gave it to your mother when you were born."

The world seemed frozen; it appeared that no birds sang outside, no breeze stirred the budding leaves of the tree outside the window. Three pairs of eyes fixed themselves on his face. What could he mean, they seemed to ask. Drawing a deep breath, he spoke:

“Diana, I believe you are my daughter.”

Chapter Thirty-six

Thalia's Letter

Diana began to cry. Minerva went to her and put her arms around her, rocking her gently and trying to soothe her with her voice and touch. Danny blurted, "Yes! I knew it when you walked in! I'm a photographer, and I earn my money looking at faces and seeking resemblances and she matches you in so many ways – coloring, manner, carriage. You have presence – you're an actor, aren't you?"

Nigel nodded his head yes, and Danny continued, "She has it too. Lots of people have commented on it. People's eyes are drawn to her when she walks into a room. But this is a terrible shock to her – to all of us!"

Minerva nodded agreement with this, and added, "She is looking for a career in theatre too! Please, can you tell us the story? We are... bewildered. Such a thing to learn!"

Nigel moved to the table where his black briefcase lay. Opening it, he pulled out a letter. Minerva recognized her mother's handwriting on the envelope, the old cursive flourishes she had learned so long ago from the nuns in the convent school. He handed it to her, saying, "She wrote this with my help when I visited her last month.

Would you like to read it aloud? It might help to hear the words rather than just see them on paper. I will leave if you would like me to."

Diana spoke for the first time since receiving this news, saying, "No. You're in this with us, I suppose, and you should be here." She looked at Minerva and Daniel and, receiving their nods of agreement, she and Nigel set the chairs in a tight cluster around the table. "Danny, you're the eldest. Would you like to begin? We can take turns."

They formed a circle, Danny between Minerva and Diana, Nigel between Diana and her sister. After a slight hesitation from Diana, they linked hands around Danny and he began to read from the letter.

"Do you remember the "Stories from Greece and Rome" that we read together? The one about Cornelia, the mother of two boys--the neighbors probably called them the Gracchi kids-- who was asked by friends to show them her jewels? Her answer was to produce her children, saying, 'These are my jewels,' and I understand exactly what Cornelia was saying. You three are my jewels. I love you all equally, and I know that each of you is a whole independent person, grown now but still for me my jewels.

Daniel, the first, the one who formed the shape of my cradling arms. There is an old belief that the lastborn child leaves his shape behind in his mother's arms, but I believe differently. I believe it was you, my first, my practice child, the one I learned on, you who shaped the cradle for your sisters who followed you. You were my consolation, my helper, my supporter. Do you remember telling me when you were very small, 'Don't worry, Mama, everything's going to be alright'? "It helped so much in those uncertain times. When Minnie arrived, you readily gave her your love, your sweetness, your care, without jealousy or demands for more attention for yourself, you just gave without stint from your loving disposition. I hope you can find someone who will want the love you give so generously, my young knight whose armor shines with love and the need to give.

And Minnie – what to say of you, child of my heart who shares my love of nature? The memory keeper, organizer, rememberer of birthdays, I know you struggle with resentment of your situation, that you are often lonely and tired, wishing for a partner and a love different from what you have found so far. But the world is changing now, old hatreds are dying, there is perhaps less prejudice in matters of love. Here in Europe you will do well, I think. There will be money to help you to shape your life to your own wants and needs, and this house as a base from which to work. If you want to keep it, fill it with plants and pets, books and music and joy. Remember Butter and Jam, the first blue-eyed cats here? They were the originals, coming to us when you were just a baby. Nefertiti and Meret are their descendants. I'm sure you will take care of them, and when they are gone I hope you will keep the tradition of blue-eyed cats, but you must do what you want.

And now the most difficult--Diana, who has just had her world drop out from beneath her. No one in the world wants to know about their parents' love lives, no one! I will try to spare you, but you need to know some things. As I'm sure Nigel has told you now (by the way, I am certain he hasn't told you that he's now Sir Nigel!), he is your father. There was room for doubt-- life was complicated in those days-- but the proof is in you, your appearance, your mannerisms, your interests. When I hear your voice, I hear his in it too. We made a difficult decision when you were born to not tell you the truth, not to deceive you but to try to give you as normal a life as possible. We both hope it was the right thing to do. But now--he wants you with him. We want you to go to London with him, where his family is waiting to welcome you as a child of their house, and where his contacts in his profession will be made available to help you as well. I hope you will go, my beloved last child, the one so different from the others, but who complements them in your own individual way.

So, to all of you, my loving goodbye. Please take my ashes to Australia and scatter them in the ocean, so that I can be part of the blueness of sea and sky, and ride the windy air with the albatross. My heart, my mind, and my love stay here with you. My voyage has ended. Yours though are just beginning. Be strong and brave! And, above all, remember to be kind.

Mama